FIRE AND FORGET

FIRE AND FORGET

by

Bob Cook

St. Martin's Press
New York

Library of Congress Cataloging-in-Publication Data

Cook, Bob.
    Fire and forget / Bob Cook.
      p.   cm.
    ISBN 0-312-05431-9
    I. Title.
  PR6053.05183F5   1991
  823′.914—dc20   90-49308
                                                     CIP

First published in Great Britain by Victor Gollancz Limited.

First U.S. Edition: January 1991
10 9 8 7 6 5 4 3 2 1

"Currently, satellites are taken care of by smart people on the surface of the earth, who watch them intensively, twenty-four hours a day. When a fault occurs, these smart people spring immediately into action. In order to put that capability into a spacecraft, it is either going to be necessary to gather these people together and take them along in the spacecraft, or to emulate their capability on board. We have programs now in artificial intelligence technology that can take expert knowledge and codify it into intelligent machines."

Robert S. Cooper
Director, US Defense Advanced Research Projects Agency
April 1985

ONE

"Full internal power."

"Twenty seconds and counting. Seventeen, sixteen . . ."

"Guidance internal."

"Twelve, eleven, ten, nine . . ."

"Engines on."

"Five, four, three . . ."

"Launch commence."

The red-painted gantry at Vandenberg Air Force Base vanished in a bright soufflé of flame. The space shuttle Atlantis slid away from Space Launch Complex 6 and roared into the Californian sky, heaved upwards by eight million pounds of rocket thrust. As the craft tore through mile after mile of the upper air, its six astronauts were jammed back on to their seats by a shuddering force equal to four times the earth's gravitational pull.

"Trajectory is good. Thrust is good."

"We copy."

"You're looking good. We're giving you a go for burn."

The booster rockets flared out and spun back towards earth, and the shuttle left the blue sky for a blacker, colder environment. Atlantis' pilots prepared themselves for the next major task: the transition to an orbit around the earth at over twenty-five thousand miles per hour.

"You are go for orbit. Go for orbit."

"Roger, that is go."

Atlantis' own engines fired for the first time, and with a gentle dip of its nose, it swung gracefully into a low polar orbit. There were no hitches, no hiccups. The shuttle's mission, codenamed Project Jacob, could now begin.

The shuttle took direct orders from the controllers at Vandenberg, but its movements were closely monitored elsewhere. Its ground track was plotted by the Space Defense Operations

Center, part of the Colorado NORAD complex. It was photographed by the GEODSS telescopes in New Mexico, South Korea and Hawaii, and its flight-path was picked out by hundreds of American-owned radars, sensors and electro-optical stations throughout the globe.

All this information was relayed to an odd-looking complex of buildings at Sunnyvale, about forty miles south of San Francisco. This was the US Air Force's Satellite Control Facility, known to its occupants as the "Big Blue Cube". And it was from here that a team of scientists supervised Project Jacob, under the command of Dr Calvin H Grant of the Defense Advanced Research Projects Agency.

Because Project Jacob was a military mission, its details were highly classified. Outside Dr Grant's circle, it was generally understood that the shuttle would place some kind of military satellite into orbit, but that was all. No other details were released to the Press, or even to the politicians. Indeed, so secret was Project Jacob that the Director of the CIA, whose job gave him total access to all his country's most sensitive information, had only the sketchiest idea of what was happening.

Of course, the Director's ignorance was wholly intentional. He did not want to know anything about Jacob until the last possible minute, in case he was summoned by a Senate committee and forced to reveal what was going on and, more importantly, how much it was costing. Project Jacob had used up over two billion dollars, and the senators may not have approved of such extravagance at a time when the US had run up a record budget deficit.

But now the shuttle was in space, and Project Jacob would soon be a *fait accompli*. The CIA Director could now afford to learn the details of the plan, and he had travelled to the Big Blue Cube for precisely this purpose. He stood beside Dr Grant in the main control room, watching a multicoloured array of oscilloscopes and video monitors manned by earnest young men and women with headphones.

"How soon?" he asked.

"Any time now," Dr Grant said. "Watch that screen there. When a yellow line appears on it, you'll know."

Dr Grant was a thin, youngish man, with a bushy moustache

8

and dreamy grey eyes. His expression was quite serene but, the CIA Director noticed, he was fidgeting nervously.

"Everything looks okay so far," the CIA Director observed. "Not that I'm in a position to judge."

"You aren't," Dr Grant smiled. "Few people are."

"How many? I mean, just who knows the details?"

"About ninety people in all," Dr Grant said. "That includes everyone here, five people at NORAD, a handful of Brass, and the Vice-President. That's it."

"Not the President?"

"Not yet. He's following your strategy. Doesn't want to know anything until Fats is up and running."

"Wise man," the CIA Director nodded.

The shuttle pilot's voice came through on a loudspeaker.

"We have parking orbit, Vandenberg. Do you read me, over?"

"Roger Atlantis, we copy. We're giving you a go for release, that is go for release."

Up in space, the shuttle's cargo bay doors opened, and a large black object floated up and out of the back of the craft. The object resembled a black Zulu shield: an ellipsoid about ten feet long and sixteen feet across. Its centre section was four feet thick, tapering off to five inches at the outer edges. As it left the cargo bay, it gradually tilted until it was hovering at a right angle to the earth's axis. Anyone watching through even the most powerful telescope would now only have seen a thin dark strip, almost invisible against the blackness of space.

Once the black object was clear of the shuttle, the cargo bay doors swung shut.

"We have release, Vandenberg."

"We confirm release, Atlantis."

"Roger. Thrusters go."

The shuttle's rockets gave a quick surge of power, and the craft began to move away from its mysterious cargo. Back at the Big Blue Cube, Dr Grant's team went into action. The men at the consoles began barking out data, checking circuitry, and activating the hardware inside the black ellipsoid.

"Height 407.235 miles and descending."

"Apogee 21,543 miles."

"Perigee 215 miles."

"Inclination 28.3 degrees."

"Parking orbit achieved."

"Confirm parking orbit."

"Test mode achieved."

"Confirm test mode."

A yellow blip appeared on the large display screen Dr Grant had indicated. It gradually stretched out into a yellow line which crept across a televised map of the earth. Dr Grant watched it in silence for several minutes. Then he clapped his hands.

"Great," he called out. "Nice work, people."

"Success?" the CIA Director enquired.

"You bet," Dr Grant said eagerly. "Fats is now in its initial, or 'parking' orbit. We'll keep it there for a few hours and then send it up to its final orbit."

"Why bother?" the CIA Director said. "I mean, why not take it to its final orbit in the first place?"

"Because," Dr Grant said patiently, "by international agreement, we have to register the parking orbits of all satellites with the United Nations."

"But not the later orbits?"

"Nope. And since our Soviet friends are waiting at the UN to hear all about this, I think the less we give away the better. Don't you?"

"Oh, sure," the CIA Director said. "Now, can you tell me what this baby does? I know that 'Fats' stands for 'Fully Autonomous Tactical Satellite', but that's all. Give me the rest."

Dr Grant took a deep breath.

"Okay," he nodded. "I don't need to tell you the importance of satellites, especially in the military sphere. Satellites carry over seventy per cent of all military communications. Also, they provide us with photoreconnaissance, weather information, signals intelligence, you name it."

"Sure."

"Basically, we'd be sunk without them. And so would the Soviets. So in time of war, the first thing each side would try to do is negate the enemy's birds."

The CIA Director blinked.

"Negate?" he repeated. "Birds?"

"Space jargon," Dr Grant said apologetically. "Satellites are known as 'birds' or 'platforms' or 'assets'. And 'to negate' means to neutralise a satellite—either by blowing it up, or pushing it out of its orbit, or by some other means."

"And everyone can do this?"

"Up to a point. Depends on the orbit, and things like that. From what we know about Russian ASAT—anti-satellite—technology, we're sure they have killer satellites that can be sent up to negate ours. Also, we're pretty certain that some of the stuff that's already up there has an ASAT capacity."

"What kind?"

"They're basically orbiting shrapnel bombs, dressed up to look like ordinary communications satellites. When one of our assets is nearby, they push the button, and our asset gets blown to pieces."

"Nasty," said the CIA Director.

"Dastardly," Dr Grant laughed. "And this is where Fats comes in. Fats is a killer satellite. Correction, Fats is *the* killer satellite. It can seek out Soviet ASATs and negate them before they do any damage to our birds. In fact, the minute hostilities begin, Fats will take out every piece of Soviet space hardware it can lay its hands on."

"I like it," the CIA Director grinned. "Hit them before they hit you."

"I believe it's known in the Pentagon as 'anticipatory retaliation'," Dr Grant said drily.

"So how does it work? You tell it that war's begun, and—"

Dr Grant shook his head.

"No we don't. Fats will know before we do. Fats will orbit the earth at a very high altitude—over sixty thousand miles—constantly scanning the planet, looking for signs of imminent conflict. It will see any missiles that are fired, any sudden movement of troops or planes or ships or subs. It will listen in to telecommunications—theirs and ours—and it will understand what's going on."

The CIA Director scratched his jaw.

"You mean this thing can understand speech? Like a person?"

"That's the idea," Dr Grant said. "And it can read text, and decode signals."

"Jesus Christ!"

"If anything happens, Fats will come down to where the action is and start fighting. It won't need any control or guidance from us. Remember, we called it the Fully Autonomous Tactical Satellite, and we weren't lying. Of all the so-called smart weapons, Fats is easily the smartest ever built."

"Incredible," the CIA Director said admiringly. "Just unbelievable. And what if Fats itself is attacked?"

"No sweat," Dr Grant said. "Remember, we hope to have at least fourteen similar machines in orbit eventually. Each of them would warn and assist the others."

"But just suppose one or two Soviet ASATs got through," the CIA Director said. "What then?"

"Fats could evade them," Dr Grant said. "Fats is very difficult to pick up on any kind of radar. It's narrow, and it's got the special ultrablack coating we used on the Stealth bomber, the kind that absorbs radar, rather than reflects it. And even if the impossible happened, and Fats got hit, well, Fats knows how to repair itself."

"You're serious?"

"Perfectly."

The CIA Director took several moments to take in the magnitude of all this. It sounded like the most extravagant brand of science fiction, and yet a respected scientist was assuring him that it was not only possible, but happening as they spoke. He stared at Dr Grant in wonder.

"This . . . this thing—" he began.

"Fats?"

"Yeah. Fats. It doesn't need orders from down here? It does everything itself? I mean, *everything*?"

"Everything," Dr Grant nodded. "At the moment it's in 'test' mode, because we want to check if it works okay. So for the next few hours it'll just do what we tell it. But once we're satisfied, and Fats is in its proper orbit, we'll put it into 'standard' mode. Then it will be fully autonomous. With just one push of our button, we can sit back and relax. Fats will take care of everything itself. You know about 'fire and forget' missiles?"

"Of course."

"Well, Fats is a fire and forget satellite. We've fired it already, and we can forget all about it until the day it's needed."

The CIA Director's face screwed up into a delighted grin, and he clicked his fingers.

"I love it," he cried. "I just love it. A fire and forget satellite. Why, that's beautiful!"

TWO

Far above the earth, in the empty, frozen darkness, Fats awoke.
Pulses of energy coursed through its optical circuits, and its brain
snapped into life. Fats' onboard supercomputer was more powerful than many thought possible: it was made of the swiftest
optical fibres and gallium arsenide chips. It stored over two
hundred billion facts, and it juggled them thirty billion times per
second.

But Fats was more than a brilliant computer. It had higher
powers: the ability to see, to recognise speech and print, to
classify patterns, track targets and gauge threats. It could assess,
enquire, learn, judge, and discuss all it knew with other machines
and people. These were the functions of minds, not computers,
and they were granted by the special brands of hardware called
neural networks: intelligent machines, modelled closely on the
human brain. Fats was now alive—deaf, dumb, blind, but alive
and thinking.

Then Fats opened its eyes: supercooled infra-red sensors, fixed
in a mosaic of glass, mirrors and prisms, which scanned the earth
through telescopic sights. Fats could see anything which radiated
heat or light—anything down to a street light or a house or a
human being. It saw in three dimensions, and with laser sharp-
ness. It read car number-plates, it recognised different makes of
aeroplanes, it followed bicycles and ships and guessed their
destinations. Above all, it watched all the world's missile sites,
looking for the tell-tale heat tracks of nuclear rocketry. From now
on, it would do this by day or night, through clear skies or cloud,
through rain, sleet and hail. It would do this for years, decades
and lifetimes, because Fats was powered by a nuclear reactor
which gave it centuries of life.

Next, Fats could hear. Its receivers trawled all the major
wavebands, sweeping up radio traffic, television signals, radar
pulses, and vital news from other satellites—all the treasure and

14

trash of telecommunication. There were a billion possible symptoms of war, and Fats was listening for all of them. It heard voices in six different languages, and understood a hundred thousand words from each. It knew the voice-prints of ten thousand of the world's mightiest soldiers and statesmen, and paid them special heed. Phone calls, chat shows, speeches, telexes: all were grist to Fats' mill.

Finally, Fats could move. Its masters at the Big Blue Cube cut the last of its electronic moorings, and Fats was free to sail for new havens in space. The booster rockets on Fats' underside belched out fifty thousand pounds of thrust, and flung the satellite far away from earth. Fats counted the distance, mile by mile, and eventually chose to slow down. Soon it found a new orbit, and its smaller hydrazine rockets, or "puffers", gently manoeuvred it into a stable position.

Fats' journey was over. It was now sixty thousand miles from home, black, silent and still. It watched its mother planet through cold, unblinking eyes. And it listened. And it waited.

THREE

Like all space shuttle missions, Project Jacob aroused widespread interest. There was much speculation about the shuttle's mysterious cargo, and the keenest of this took place in the Soviet Union. From the moment Atlantis took off from Vandenberg, much of the Soviet radar system was focused upon the spacecraft and its activities.

At Abalakovo, near Krasnoyarsk in central Siberia, the USSR's most powerful tracking station picked up the strange black satellite and tried to guess its purpose. Leading the investigation was the cheerful portly figure of Professor Arkady Kamenev, of the Soviet Academy of Sciences.

Professor Kamenev was a red-faced, vigorous man with curly grey hair, wire-framed spectacles and a deep, sonorous voice. His working methods were simple, but effective. He gathered the brightest young scientists available, and with a combination of shouts, derision and extravagant praise, he coaxed out their best ideas.

His people were deeply puzzled by the information they were receiving. After several hours of investigation, Professor Kamenev took them to a conference room to pool their theories.

"Right, my children," he bellowed. "Your thoughts, please."

He lit a small cigar and waved his hand in invitation. The scientists looked at each other uncomfortably.

"Definitely a satellite," one of them muttered.

"Oh, that's good," Professor Kamenev said impatiently. "That's very good. I *know* it's a satellite, Rudi. Come on, my children. Think!"

"A new surveillance platform," another one guessed. "But it has a completely different cross-section from anything they've sent up before."

"Unusual radar signature," another agreed. "So faint we can hardly catch it."

"That's deliberate, obviously," Kamenev said. "But why go to all this trouble to disguise a camera? It must be more than just a photoreconnaissance platform."

"Some kind of ABM device, then," someone suggested. "A piece of Star Wars hardware they're testing."

"Yes, Nadia," Kamenev nodded approvingly. "That sounds more like it. A laser platform, perhaps. Have we any pictures yet, Tolya?"

"Just this, Professor. From the observatory at Pulkovo."

The Professor was given two glossy prints showing a blurred black strip against a grey blackground. To the naked eye, the pictures looked identical. In fact, each was taken from a slightly different position. Together they could be used to form a stereo-scopic image, from which computers could calculate the size and depth of the curious black object.

"A near ellipse," Kamenev observed. "Quite large, for a satellite."

"But it doesn't look like a laser platform," Rudi objected.

"Doesn't look like anything at all," Tolya said.

Kamenev blew out a cloud of smoke and smiled ruefully.

"Quite so," he sighed. "A beautiful design. That's why we're struggling to keep track of it, children. You notice there are no bulges, no extra curves, nothing to reflect radar. It must have lenses, but they've hidden them. And if it carried its own booster rockets, they're buried deep inside. Everything's sunk back into the machine. It's a masterpiece, whatever it does."

"But what *does* it do?"

The Academician shrugged.

"What are the options, children? Some kind of early-warning radar? Maybe, maybe not. A laser gun? Maybe, maybe not. What else?"

"An ASAT device?" Nadia said.

Kamenev frowned.

"What sort of ASAT device?"

"I . . . I don't know."

"*Think*, woman!"

"An . . . an orbiting bomb?" Rudi offered. "Like our FOBS cluster weapons, perhaps."

Kamenev pursed his lips and made a farting noise.

17

"We need more data," he decided. "We can only see this end of the machine, because that's all they want us to see. That means another view—from directly over it, perhaps—will give something more away."

The intercom buzzed, and Kamenev scowled at it.

"Yes?"

"I think you should know, Professor. The satellite has disappeared."

"What?"

"It's changed orbit, and we've lost radar contact. The observatory can still see it, though, and they say it's heading out."

"Geosynchronous orbit?"

"Further, Professor."

The scientists looked at each other curiously.

"Fascinating," Kamenev declared. "Is that all?"

"No, Professor. Marshal Zhdanov is on the line. He wants to speak to you urgently."

"Well, well," Kamenev grinned. "My dear old friend Zhdanov. I wonder what he wants."

The professor was being sarcastic. Marshal Zhdanov was the Soviet Union's formidable Chief of Defence, and he was nobody's dear old friend. He was a tempestuous old gentleman, who spent much of his time raging at the perceived failings of those around him. Zhdanov detested Kamenev, because the professor was one of the few people he could not bawl into submission. In Marshal Zhdanov's view, Kamenev was an obstreperous insect who had no right to be in charge of anything. The feelings were entirely mutual.

"My dear Marshal," Kamenev said genially. "It's delightful to hear from you. And what can we do for you today?"

"You can cut out that bullshit for starters," Zhdanov said. "What's that fucking satellite for, eh?"

"We've no idea, Marshal," Kamenev admitted.

"I might have known," Zhdanov said. "You're useless, absolutely useless."

"I'm afraid we lack the necessary information, Marshal."

"Horse shit. You lack the necessary brains. I've got more scientific know-how in my cock than you have in your whole team. Bunch of useless dilettantes, that's what you are."

"You're too kind, Marshal."

"Kinder than you deserve, Kamenev. Now listen: the entire defence staff are rushing around like headless chickens. We need to know what that thing is, see? That's what we're paying your limp-wristed pansies for. If you don't know, I want all the possibilities. All of them, Kamenev. And if I don't get them by tonight, I'll personally shove your balls through the mincer. Understand?"

Professor Kamenev shook his head sadly, and took another puff from his cigar.

"Comrade Marshal," he said, "I can understand why you're such a foul-mouthed oaf—"

"*What?*"

"—after all, you were the head of the KGB for a while, and they're all scum, as we know. But you've left them now, and I suggest you try to acquire some of the traits of normal, civilised people."

"Why you—"

"Believe me Marshal," Kamenev said solemnly, "it can be done. They can train monkeys to do it, so even former KGB chiefs shouldn't pose too much of a challenge."

"You fucking snotball, Kamenev! I've a good mind to—"

"No, Marshal. You haven't a good mind. You've no mind at all. I'll send you our findings when I'm good and ready. Goodbye."

Kamenev turned off the intercom and looked round at his assistants.

"Well, my children," he said. "You heard the good Marshal. He wants all our theories. And since he asks so nicely, how can we possibly refuse?"

FOUR

"I still can't believe this machine is so smart," the CIA Director said.

"You'll get used to the idea," Dr Grant promised. "Fats sounds pretty awesome—new developments always do. But in a few years' time, they'll be making consumer items using the same technology. I guarantee it."

The CIA Director shrugged.

"Maybe, but I'm still impressed. What gets me is how you managed to pull off this whole project without anyone finding out. That was the really smart thing."

Dr Grant waved his hand airily.

"Easy," he said. "We just put Fats together using components and ideas from other projects. Fats' shell, for example: that's an alloy of titanium and beryllium developed by some genius at Lockheed for an experimental aircraft. We just stole the formula. The ultrablack coating comes from the Northrop B-2 bomber. The supercomputer was designed by some researchers at Cornell University. Other stuff comes from NASA, some from the Rockwell Science Center—you name it, we've scrounged it. Fats is really one big mongrel."

The CIA Director laughed.

"But it's so damned *good*," he said. "How can it do all this? I mean, Fats isn't just a computer, is it? It can teach itself things. It understands human conversation. Computers can't do that, can they?"

Dr Grant shook his head.

"No. Computers are just adding machines. If you want to teach them anything, you have to give them elaborate rules. The computer follows the rule—no more, and no less. In fact, computers are pretty dumb."

"So how does Fats learn things?"

"The way humans do. We get the hang of new skills by

constant trial and error. When children are learning to speak their language, they don't ask what every single new word means. They just use the word, and if they get it wrong, they see that nobody understands. If they use the word properly, people do understand. It's the same with most things people learn: they get it right a few times, wrong a few times, and finally they master it. That's how Fats was trained."

The CIA Director nodded.

"I see. So if Fats' brain isn't a computer, what is it?"

Dr Grant smiled.

"Something called a neural network," he said. "Basically, they're machines which work the way neurons do in the brain, complete with somas, dendrites and synapses. To put it crudely, if a machine resembles a brain, it should be capable of doing whatever a brain can do."

"And whose idea was this?"

"Oh, a lot of people. The theory's been around for years. Most research is still fairly primitive. But luckily for us, one guy took it much further than everyone else. He was a really brilliant man, Mr Director. A true original. A lot of his hardware is up there inside Fats."

"Who is this guy?"

"An Englishman, called Clement Fairbrother. He worked at the MIT Lincoln Laboratory in Lexington. You should see the things he did there, Mr Director. All of it was genius."

"You said 'was'. What happened to him?"

"Sad story. He was working for the Defense Department, you understand, so all his work was classified. Fairbrother worked alone, and he seldom discussed his job with anybody. It drove him slightly crazy. He had a nervous breakdown some time back, so they gave him six months off work. He went back to England to recover, but he never returned. Burned out, I guess."

"Damned shame," the CIA Director said.

"Tragedy," Dr Grant agreed. "He was a likeable guy, too. I often wonder what happened to him."

FIVE

When most people think of London, they think of the big city on the north side of the river Thames. All the best-known parts lie north of the river: the City, Parliament, Covent Garden, the Tower, Buckingham Palace, Trafalgar Square and Hyde Park. South of the Thames is seldom thought about, and with good reason. It has few tourist attractions and consists largely of housing. Some of it is pleasant, much of it is ugly, but none of it is particularly exciting.

From time to time, there have been attempts to change this state of affairs. They have all failed. The most spectacular failure of all was the South Bank complex, which runs between the Hungerford and Blackfriars bridges. This is a confusing jumble of modernist buildings made of sooty grey concrete, which houses theatres, a museum, concert halls and galleries, all linked by a series of cracked walkways and grimy terraces.

The complex was intended to be London's *rive gauche*, and the planners hoped it would prompt an economic revival in the depressed borough of Lambeth. It has done nothing of the sort. The theatre-goers and music lovers do come to the South Bank, but they are seldom tempted to stray beyond it. There has been no economic renaissance in Lambeth, and the complex remains what it always was: a concrete archipelago.

But not everyone has rejected the South Bank. One group of citizens is closely associated with the place. These are the homeless men and women who spend their nights in boxes beneath the concrete walkways, and who shuffle along the paths and terraces by day. Their community is known as Cardboard City, and they are the only full-time residents of the South Bank complex.

By day, it is easy not to notice these people. Many are elsewhere, in search of work, food and alcohol. Those who remain lie slumped along the paths and benches, and some accost passers-by for change, but most blend into the affluent throng of tourists and entertainment seekers.

It is only at night, when the visitors have gone back to their indoor homes, that all the Cardboard Citizens come home to rest. Then the lower levels of the South Bank become an open-air tramps' hostel, littered with bottles, boxes and broken people.

One damp April evening, there was a new arrival at Cardboard City. He looked much like any other resident: grimy, ragged, and old before his time. He was perhaps slightly better fed than most, and his eyes were a little more bright and alert. But his face was grey and chapped, his shoulders sagged, and he did not stand out from the crowd.

The man did not have a cardboard box, so he sat beside a concrete pillar and covered himself in newspapers. Then he looked over his surroundings. Ten feet to his left, a man and woman shared a bottle of sherry and a slurred conversation about nothing in particular. A little further on, a group of young men were dozing in tattered sleeping bags. Beside them, an old madman was conducting a heated debate with himself, and appeared to be losing the argument. His babblings were over-heard by a pair of Irishmen, who found them mildly entertaining. Elsewhere, in the darker recesses, other people snored and groaned and broke wind. The only coherent discussion came from three men to the newcomer's right, who had strong but divergent views on the subject of philanthropy.

"You help your pals, right?" said one of them, a large purple-faced Scot in his late thirties. "Should always help your pals. When you can. But you got to put yourself first. Number one, right?"

"Oh, definitely."

The Scotsman took a long pull from a bottle of cider.

"Can't help others if you can't help yourself, right?"

The second man nodded solemnly. He was well into middle age, with a sick yellow face and trembling hands.

"Definitely, Craig," he said, taking the bottle. "But it's only number one that counts. You can't really trust any chap except yourself, can you? Other people let you down in the end. Always."

23

He spoke in a surprisingly cultured voice, and his hand movements were those of the chairman of a board.

"Not always," the third man disagreed. "Not everybody's selfish."

He was the youngest of the three, barely out of his teens, and he spoke with the flat vowels of northern England. His hair was cropped short and dyed in a variety of lurid colours. There was a line of gold studs in his ear.

"You have to trust other people sometimes," he added.

"Right," said Craig the Scotsman.

"Not if I can help it," the second man grinned. "That's just asking for trouble."

"Right," Craig agreed.

"Why?" the third man demanded. "People aren't all bastards, you know. Some are all right."

"Yeah, some are," Craig admitted.

"Well, I've never met them," the second man said.

"Oh come on, Miles," the young man groaned. "What about the soup van? Every night, half-past eleven, they come here and give us bread and soup. They don't want money, they don't want thanks. They're good people."

The second man, Miles, was unimpressed.

"Oh yes," he scoffed. "Angels. I wonder what their racket is."

"Racket? What are you talking about?"

"Really, Spider," Miles said sorrowfully. "Wake up, will you? You really think they come to this dump every night and feed us just for the joy of doing good? They get grants for doing it, old boy. Hard cash."

"Right," Craig agreed.

"So what?" Spider said. "Someone's got to pay for it."

"Certainly. But who says all the money goes where it should? Who says they aren't creaming off a quarter of the grant—half, even—and slipping it into their own pockets?"

"I don't believe it," Spider said.

"You should, old boy. Have you seen their account books? Of course not."

"Nor have you," Spider objected.

"Why else would they do the work?" Miles reasoned. "What would be the point? I'd much rather be at home with the wife—"

"Giving her one," Craig grinned.

"—than hanging around here. Wouldn't you? Wouldn't any sane man?"

Spider shrugged.

"Well, I'd be happy to work on the soup van."

"Nonsense."

"I would."

"Yes," Miles sighed. "Perhaps you would, at that. There are one or two bleeding-heart do-gooders around, I admit. But no normal person would do that sort of work without an added incentive. What do you think, old boy?"

He glanced towards the newcomer, who had followed the conversation with interest. The man was mildly taken aback by the question, and he gave a perplexed shrug.

"Don't really know. Someone has to do it, I suppose."

"Nobody *has* to," Spider said. "But they should."

"You're new here, aren't you?" Craig observed. "Haven't seen you before."

The newcomer nodded.

"I stayed in King's Cross for a few days. One of the hostels. But my money's run out, and I won't get any more till tomorrow. They said they couldn't help until then."

Miles smiled sourly.

"You mean they *wouldn't* help. Bastards. They're all the same, those people."

"Right," Craig nodded.

"Some are all right," Spider objected.

The newcomer realised the conversation had come full circle.

"My name's Clement Fairbrother," he said.

"Pleased to meet you, Clem," Miles said, and the three men introduced themselves.

Craig was an ex-convict from Edinburgh, who had served several terms for violence. For a while he had made his living in the illegal boxing tournaments in East London, but he was forced to stop when alcohol dulled his reflexes.

Miles was a former businessman, who had gone bankrupt. Unable to start again from scratch, he had taken to drink, and his wife left him. Shortly afterwards his home was repossessed and he found himself in Cardboard City.

Spider was from Preston in Lancashire. Like many of his age, he had come to London in search of work. All he could get was an occasional living as a rent-boy, and most of his earnings were spent on drugs and junk food. But unlike the others, he still carried a spark of optimism, and he had yet to be crippled by drink.

"What about you?" Miles enquired. "What were you before you came here? A male model? Airline pilot? Brain surgeon?"

"I was a computer scientist," Clem said.

The others roared with laughter.

"That's a good one," Craig said.

"It's true," Clem insisted. "I worked for the US Defense Department."

His new friends found this richly entertaining.

"Anything you say, old boy," Miles grinned. "You know, we had one chap who claimed he'd been the President of a South American junta."

Clem stared.

"And was he?"

"Anything's possible," Miles shrugged. "I mean, even a Generalissimo might speak English with a Dublin accent. But it's a little unlikely, don't you think?"

SIX

"Okay, Mr President?" asked the make-up girl. She held a mirror before the American President's face.

"Great," he nodded. "Maybe a little more powder on the nose, huh?"

"Sure thing," she said, dabbing her powder-puff on the President's proboscis.

"How about the highlights?" he asked thoughtfully. "You think they're okay?"

"Fine," she said. "Look in the monitor, Mr President. You're just right."

The President glanced down at the TV screen which the camera crew had obligingly placed beside his desk.

"Yeah," he decided. "We'll leave it there. Thanks, honey."

The make-up girl left, and the President took another look at the monitor. He straightened his tie, and practised his smile. It was a big, white professional smile, perfected over many years. Before arriving at the White House, the President had made his living by performing in toothpaste commercials on television. His was probably the best known mouth in America, and it had taken him to the highest office in the land.

Today the President's smile would be used to charm the crew of the space shuttle Atlantis, who would be listening at Edwards Air Force Base within the hour. The President's busy schedule precluded a personal visit to the landing site, but he would greet the astronauts via a live TV link-up from the Oval Office, and offer them his congratulations for a job well done.

After releasing Fats, the shuttle team had orbited the earth for a further three days and conducted a range of scientific experiments. Most of this work was of limited value, but it offered camouflage for Project Jacob, since it implied that there were other reasons for making the trip. However, none of this would be mentioned in the broadcast, which was little more than an exercise in public relations.

"How are you doing, Mr President?" the TV director asked.

The President was peering at the autocue, which contained his prepared speech.

"'My fellow astronauts'," he read. "Is that right? Sounds weird, somehow. Oh well. 'Never in the field of space exploration have so many owed so much to—'"

"You ready, Mr President?" the director persisted.

The President looked up.

"Oh great, great," he said. "Hunky-dory. When are we on the air?"

"Real soon, Mr President. I think we've got our link-up now."

The director went over to consult with his technical team, one of whom was having some difficulties with his equipment.

"We've got pictures," the man said, "but I'm not sure about sound."

"Can we hear them?"

"Yeah, definitely. But I don't know if they can hear us. Hello? Anyone out there?"

"It's the dishes upstairs," the director grimaced. "Lousiest equipment I've ever seen."

The director was referring to the microwave dishes on the roof of the White House. In fact, the dishes were perfectly sound; it was the security team who frequently dislodged them when patrolling the roof.

"That gear's fine," the sound man said. "I had it checked out an hour ago. It could just be this mike."

"In that case, let's use the main one," the director suggested, and he waved his hand at the President. "Excuse me, Mr President, could you try out your microphone for us?"

"Sure thing," the President said affably. "What do you want me to say?"

"Anything you like, Mr President. Just talk into the mike."

The President hesitated. He disliked doing anything without a script. Even a simple sound check was a daunting prospect, if his team of speech writers was not there to guide him through it.

"Relax, Mr President," the director said encouragingly. "Just say whatever's in your mind."

The President frowned. That was not a helpful suggestion. There was seldom anything in his mind—another secret of his political success. He struggled desperately to think of something, any simple banality, but nothing would come.

Fortunately, the President had only recently been elected, and the campaign was still fresh in his thoughts. He remembered a simple rule given to him by one of his handlers: whenever he was at a loss for a reply to a question, or a sharp debating point from his opponent, he should crack a joke. People loved jokes.

"All right," the President grinned. "How about this, guys? My fellow Americans. It is my sad duty to inform you that we are now at war with the Soviet Union. We will soon be bombing Russia. I will shortly give the order, and we will nuke Moscow—"

"Jesus Christ!" the director exclaimed.

"It's working," the sound man yelped. "The mike's working!"

"Turn it off!"

"At this very moment, the Strategic Air Command is—"

"Mr President, stop! Please!"

The President blinked innocently.

"Something wrong?"

"We were on the air, Mr President."

"No kidding?"

"I mean live, Mr President. Millions of people heard you."

"Gee. You sure about that?"

The director closed his eyes and shuddered.

"Positive," he whispered.

The President grinned sheepishly, and flapped his hand.

"Aw, hell. They won't mind. Switch the mike back on."

The director hesitated.

"Go ahead," the President said confidently. "I can handle it."

The director turned to the sound man and nodded.

"Hello again, my fellow Americans," the President said. "Now, some of you may be worried by what you just heard. Well, don't be. *It's all true.*"

He gave a broad wink into the camera, and his lips formed a roguish leer. The camera crew laughed loudly, and even the director permitted himself a smile. The crisis was over as quickly as it had begun.

The director shook his head in admiration. Whatever his faults, the President was a master of the camera. Nobody could dislike so genial a man. He really was one in a million.

SEVEN

Sixty thousand miles above the Pacific Ocean, Fats heard the call. There was no other traffic on that frequency, and the signal was sharp and unbroken. At once, Fats' reasoning faculties got to work.

Firstly, the voice. There was no mistaking it. Fats carried thousands of samples of that voice in its data banks, and there was no doubt about who it belonged to: the Commander-in-Chief of all US forces. If confirmation was needed, Fats knew the signal came directly from the roof of the White House. The odds against two men with identical voice-prints standing in the same building were in the order of many billions to one. There could be no coincidence.

Furthermore, there were two distinct broadcasts. The first one made the announcement, and was then cut off. Moments later, it was confirmed by a second transmission. This ruled out a slip of the tongue, or any other kind of accident.

Thirdly, the message was unambiguous. The United States was at war with the Soviet Union. Orders had been sent out to SAC, the Strategic Air Command, to attack Moscow. Precisely when this would happen was not clear: the message said that Moscow would be bombed "soon", which could mean anything. But the exact timetable was of little concern to Fats. All it needed to know was that war had been declared, and this message had got through loud and clear.

Just what had prompted this war was a mystery to Fats. There was no hint of impending conflict in any of the broadcasts Fats had picked up over the last seventy-two hours. And Fats had seen no unusual military activity on either side of the Iron Curtain.

Fats continued to scan the surface of the earth for signs of the new war, but nothing could be seen. This was not particularly surprising, however. If the United States had chosen to launch a

31

pre-emptive strike, for whatever reason, it would obviously do so at the quietest possible time, when the enemy was least prepared. There would be no warnings of any kind, and Fats would expect to see none.

But if this was a pre-emptive strike, the Americans were conducting it in a surprisingly relaxed manner. Fats could see no signs of the SAC bombers, or the heat trails from American missile silos. Of course, even though war had been declared, it was possible that the nuclear bombing was merely some form of bluff, designed to persuade the Soviet Union to surrender immediately. Once again, the details did not interest Fats. Whatever the United States' strategy, it was always possible that the Soviets would launch their own retaliatory nuclear strike, and Fats had to be ready for it.

Thus, it was time for Fats to swoop down from its faraway perch in space. Many miles below, the enemy was waiting. Fats' puffer rockets tilted it into a new angle, and with one giant blast from its main booster, the killer satellite went down to do battle.

EIGHT

"What happened, Jack?" Dr Grant demanded.

"Search me," his assistant said. "All we know for sure is that Fats is coming down."

Dr Grant stared at the big video display, where Fats' path was shown as a yellow line. At a certain point, the line turned orange, indicating downward movement. Finally it went bright red, which meant a rapid descent. All around the main control room in the Big Blue Cube, the scientists stood by their consoles and worked feverishly to stop the runaway satellite. At the same time, one of them read out Fats' height.

"Fifty thousand . . . forty-seven thousand . . . forty-five thousand and falling . . ."

"We've tried everything," Jack said. "Direct commands, EHF frequency-hopping—"

"Okay, relax," Dr Grant said. "Have you gone through all the last orders Fats received from you?"

"Sure. I've re-read the last hundred commands. There's nothing wrong there. And even if there was one freak command, it wouldn't be enough to achieve this. Fats would always query a bum order."

"Forty thousand and falling."

"No response of any kind from Fats' transmitter?" Dr Grant asked.

"None whatsoever. It's blacked out. I mean, it's just as if we told it go into 'active' mode."

"Thirty-eight thousand."

Dr Grant's eyes widened.

"But that's exactly what it's done, Jack. It's gone into 'active'. Christ! Have you phoned NORAD?"

"Well, no—"

"Do it! Don't you see? If we're at war, Fats is going to know long before we do."

33

Jack paled, and ran off to the nearest telephone. Dr Grant called out for attention, and his scientists turned towards him.

"Listen, guys," he said. "This is probably just a glitch. But there's an outside chance that Fats is doing its job properly, and it may have seen something we haven't. We'll know for sure in a minute. In the meantime, I want you to try everything you can to ask Fats why it's coming down. Don't try to stop it: I just want to know what caused this, okay?"

The scientists returned to their consoles and began sending up a variety of messages on a wide range of frequencies. Some were in continuous code, others went up in short electronic "squirts", and others were sent by laser. All failed to elicit any reply.

"Thirty-two thousand . . . thirty thousand . . ."

Jack rushed back into the control room, shaking his head. All the scientists listened for his news.

"You'll be pleased to hear we aren't at war," he grinned. "NORAD says everything's quiet, and what the hell do we mean by giving them a fright like that?"

Dr Grant laughed.

"Well, that's good to know. But in that case, why the hell is Fats on 'active'?"

"Maybe it got bored with the view," someone joked.

"Yeah," someone else added, "and maybe it decided to start World War Three, just to liven things up a little."

Dr Grant closed his eyes.

"Don't," he said imploringly. "Don't even think about it."

Over at the Krasnoyarsk radar station, Dr Kamenev's people were equally perturbed by Fats' behaviour. Fats was not yet within range of their radars, but pictures from the Pulkovo observatory showed that Fats would soon be down to a more visible height. Tolya was on the phone to the observatory, and he called out each new height reading as it came in.

"Twenty-seven thousand, and falling."

Dr Kamenev glanced at a blank video monitor, and frowned in perplexity.

"What do you make of it, my children? First she goes up to the middle of nowhere; now she comes tearing down to earth. What are the Americans playing at?"

"Some kind of test, presumably," Rudi said. "They're trying to see how quickly they can change her orbit."

"In that case," Kamenev said, "why didn't they do this two days ago? What have they been waiting for?"

"Twenty-five thousand miles and descending," Tolya noted. "Maybe she's heading for geosynchronous orbit."

"We'll soon know. Is she giving anything off? Microwave? Laser?"

"No laser, Professor."

"Or microwave."

"Fifteen thousand, now. That's well below geosynchronous."

Professor Kamenev trimmed a cigar and popped it into his mouth.

"Any minute now," he said.

A blip suddenly appeared on the monitor, as Fats came within range of the radars. Fat' main rocket gave off enough heat to allow the infra-red sensors to get a fix.

"If there's no microwave," Professor Kamenev said thoughtfully, "it means she isn't sending any data back home. So it can't be a test."

"She's not being guided either, as far as we can tell," Nadia said.

Professor Kamenev's eyes popped.

"And therefore . . . she's working on her own! This is an autonomous satellite!"

The scientists fell silent. This was news. The Americans had fully automatic satellites, capable of guiding themselves around space. Such satellites had long been forecast, but none had ever been built.

Professor Kamenev lit his cigar and sat down.

"Right, my children. We know what she is. The next question is, what's she for? Communications? Surveillance?"

"Maybe nothing," Tolya said. "Maybe this is a non-functioning prototype. Once they've perfected her, they'll give her something to do."

"Unlikely," Kamenev muttered. "As we said, this is no test. Otherwise they'd be taking data from it. No, my children, this is a functioning machine."

35

"She's flattening out," Tolya announced. "She must be heading for a new orbit."

"Give me the figures."

Tolya wrote down a string of numbers, and tapped them into a nearby computer terminal. Seconds later, the computer worked out the precise orbit into which Fats was manoeuvring itself, and printed it out. Tolya tore off the paper and handed it to Kamenev.

"Well, well," the Professor said. "Give me the phone, Tolya. Hello? Put me through to the Defence Ministry, please. I want Marshal Zhdanov . . ."

There was a pause, and Kamenev's eyes twinkled in anticipation.

"Hello? Marshal Zhdanov?"

"Speaking," Zhdanov barked. "What do you want, Kamenev? I'm busy."

"I just thought you'd like to know, Marshal. The mystery satellite is autonomous."

"Come again?"

"She's wholly automatic, Marshal. She runs herself."

There was a deep hiss at the other end of the line.

"Are you sure about this, Kamenev? This isn't another of your fuck-ups? I've had it up to here with your shit-for-brains Academy boys and their theories—"

"There's no doubt, Marshal. I'd stake my reputation on it."

"Is that supposed to impress me?" Zhdanov said. "Anyway, send me all the data at once. Now, if that's all—"

"It isn't."

Marshal Zhdanov took a deep breath.

"Go on."

"The satellite has just come down to a new orbit."

"So what?"

"A low orbit, Marshal."

"Well? Who gives a fuck?"

"You should, Marshal. You see, the American machine is in the same orbit range as our own military satellites."

Marshal Zhdanov took the point. His voice dropped by several decibels, and it began to sound almost reasonable.

"All right, Kamenev. Thank you for telling me."

36

"My pleasure, Marshal. I should point out that we expect to lose track of her soon."

"Why?"

"Once she's in her new orbit, her main booster will shut down. There'll be no infra-red signature, so our radars will be useless. What she does then will be anybody's guess. If she's over our territory, our observatories may catch sight of her. If not . . ."

"I understand," Zhdanov said. "Very well: you'd better come to Moscow."

"Tonight?"

"Right away. We've got work to do."

NINE

Clem awoke. He blinked and yawned and wondered where he was. Then he remembered: St Benedict's, the big hostel in Westminster. The weather had turned cold and very wet, and Cardboard City had to be abandoned for a while. Fortunately, Clem's money had come through, and with his three new friends, he found temporary shelter in this crumbling old building.

St Benedict's was not too bad, as hostels went. It was cold and dirty, and like most accommodation for the homeless, it stank like a drain. But for two pounds a night, Clem had his own cubicle to sleep in, with a couple of threadbare blankets and a hard boxwood bed.

He sat up and dressed, looking over each item of clothing before he put it on. It was surprising how quickly even the best garments wore out when you lived in the streets. Clem had never been a dandy, but he dressed well. His tweed jacket came from Savile Row, his shoes were hand-lasted, and his shirt and trousers were from reputable firms in America. All had been made to last, and all let him down. The jacket was now oily with dirt, and the elbows had worn through. His shoes let in rainwater, and were stuffed with cardboard. His trousers were falling apart, and his shirt was frayed and stiff with sweat. *Sic transit gloria*, Clem thought, and he smiled ruefully.

It was all so different from what he was used to. Not that Clem saw himself as a special case: he knew that plenty had fallen from even greater heights, and there were depths he had yet to fathom. But this did not soften the shock of his new existence. Every day brought some new revelations about the world, or about Clem himself, and he wondered how he could have spent fifty-seven years on this planet without noticing any of it.

He stepped out into the corridor. Most of the other cubicles were empty, and the bedding was dumped in the hallway. Some of the sheets had been fouled by their users, and the linoleum floor glistened with pools of urine. Clem tiptoed through the mess, and made his way downstairs to get his breakfast.

The dining hall was big and loud, and seated over five hundred. Most people sat in sullen silence at the long tables, but some formed groups and held noisy, disjointed conversations. In one corner, a trio of punks shared a raucous joke at the expense of an old man. Elsewhere, two men were comparing their artificial limbs. At another table, a man was hitting himself on the jaw with steady, rhythmical blows. A woman nearby swore violently at an overhead light bulb. The man behind her was covered in cuts and dried blood, but he found something to giggle about hysterically. And a few feet away, Miles, Craig and Spider were calmly eating their breakfast.

Clem went over to the serving area, and was given a cup of sweet tea, a bowl of grey porridge, and a plate of sausage and beans. Two slices of bread and margarine were tossed on to his tray, and he was sent on his way. He sat down with his friends, who greeted him affably.

"All right?" Craig inquired.

"Fine, thank you," Clem nodded.

"You slept well," Spider observed. "We were up an hour ago."

"I hardly got a wink," Miles complained. "The man in the next cubicle had a fight with someone else. His boyfriend, I think. They were screwing each other half the night, which was noisy enough. Then they had a row, and the boyfriend beat the shit out of him."

"Why?" Clem asked.

"How should I know?" Miles shrugged. "That's what they're like."

"Fucking poofs," Craig grunted.

"How peculiar," Clem said. "Didn't somebody stop them?"

"Eventually," Miles said. "One of the staff came round, and threw them both out. But by then it was six o'clock. Noisy bastards."

Clem gave a baffled frown, as if this was an abstract mathematical conundrum.

"Why?" he repeated. "What purpose does any of it serve?"

"No purpose at all," Spider laughed.

"No purpose?" Clem blinked. "Surely there's a *reason*—"

"It's these places," Spider said. "They bring out the worst in everyone."

"Right," Craig nodded.

"Does the sty make the pig, or the pig the sty?" Miles said. "You wouldn't believe it, but this place was even worse six months ago, before they redecorated it."

"They spent thousands repainting it," Craig said. "Thousands. But I can't see any difference."

"They wasted the money," Spider said. "They always waste money, those people."

"Who?" Clem asked. "The hostel owners?"

"Sure," Spider nodded. "Hostel owners. Local councils. Governments. They always chuck money away. Look at all the millions they spend on defence. Millions and millions, and it's a lot of bollocks."

"I can't agree, old boy," Miles said. "You have to have armies. It's unavoidable."

"Maybe," Spider conceded. "But what about all those fancy weapons? Half of them are just for show. All those homing rockets that never bloody work right—what do you call them? Clever missiles, or something."

"Smart weapons," Clem said.

"That's right. What's the bloody use of them?"

"If the other side's got them, we need them too," Miles said.

"Yeah, that's the excuse," Spider sneered. "You're always talking about rackets. Well, there's a real racket for you. All that money should go on better things."

"You're right there," Craig said. "Homes for people like us."

Miles shook his head firmly.

"There's no point in having homes," he said, "if you can't defend them properly."

"I'm not saying we shouldn't have defence," Spider retorted. "Just spend the money better, that's all. They waste millions, those people."

"Billions," Clem agreed. "And I should know."

Miles grinned mischievously, and licked the last of the porridge off his spoon.

"Ah yes," he said. "The defence computer man. I'd forgotten

40

about that. I suppose you had a big budget at your disposal, in your time."

"Oh yes," Clem nodded. "Several million dollars, at one stage. And I can tell you, Spider's right. Much of that money would be better spent elsewhere."

"And that's why you chucked it in and joined our merry band, I suppose. All that extravagance was too much for you."

"No," Clem said. "Not exactly."

"Lay off him, Miles," Spider said.

"In that case," Miles continued, "how did you fall from grace? Let me guess: your conscience broke down. You couldn't bear to see your brilliant talents used to make weapons of destruction. You're a man of peace, an idealist—"

"Shut up, for Christ's sake," Craig groaned.

"What's the matter?" Miles said innocently. "If Clem really was a scientist, and he isn't just telling us the plot from the last film he saw, he should be able to answer my question. Shouldn't you Clem?"

Clem took a sip of his tea, and nodded calmly.

"Good," Miles said brightly. "So what happened to you, then? Did you get a sudden attack of pacifism?"

"No," Clem said. "Nothing like that. I have no qualms about my work. It was worthwhile, even if it was done for the military. I . . . I just had to leave, that's all."

"Are you on the run?" Craig asked.

Clem glanced at him sharply.

"Why do you ask?"

"No reason," Craig shrugged.

"A mystery man," Miles laughed. "This gets better and better."

Clem pushed away his plate, and rested his chin on his hands.

"You're wrong, Miles," he said thoughtfully. "It gets worse and worse. And I don't know how it's going to end."

TEN

Fats was spoilt for choice. There were dozens of possible targets in space—hundreds, if one counted all the floating bric-à-brac from past projects. But Fats was not interested in the old machines. It wanted the latest Soviet hardware, for that was where the real threat lay. And it was not too long before Fats found what it was seeking: a silvery-blue cylinder flying a south-north polar track, two hundred miles above the United States.

Fats consulted its data banks, and its suspicions were confirmed. This was a Cosmos 2802, the latest brand of Soviet photoreconnaissance satellite. Like most Soviet platforms, it was a modified Soyuz space capsule. It was twenty-three feet long, seven feet in diameter, and weighed seven tons. The crew module carried film canisters instead of cosmonauts, the equipment module was filled with fuel, and the spherical compartment at the front housed the cameras which scanned America's cities, roads and military installations. It was the perfect target.

In less than a second, Fats' computer worked out the necessary course for a successful kill. First, Fats had to change its inclination to match that of the Cosmos craft. Then, over the course of several journeys round the earth, Fats would gradually change its own track until it flew alongside the target satellite, keeping fifty feet above it in a "grazing" orbit. The whole process would take about three hours. After that, the Cosmos would be at Fats' mercy.

Down at the Big Blue Cube, Dr Grant watched these developments with mounting alarm.

"It's homing in on something," he said. "Do we know what?"

"A Cosmos satellite," Jack said. "At least, that's what Space Command think. There's no other likely target in that range of orbits."

One of the team looked up from his oscilloscope.

42

"Yeah, it's definitely the Russky," he said. "Fats is on course for a grazing orbit in three minutes."

"Then what?" Dr Grant demanded.

The scientist shrugged.

"Then," he suggested, "Fats will sing the last chorus from *South Pacific* and perform a triple somersault. Or something."

"Or something," Dr Grant agreed. "Still no response to any of our signals?"

"None. I tell you, Cal, we've just about exhausted the possibilities. Those neural networks seem to have taken complete control. Nothing we say makes any impression on that sonofabitch."

Dr Grant thought about this.

"Okay," he decided. "In that case, then we should try to by-pass the neural networks. If enough signals are sent straight to the computer, they might override the commands from—"

"Too late for that," Jack said quickly. "Look at the screen. Fats is kicking ass."

Fats was indeed creating mayhem in space. Having aligned itself with the Cosmos satellite, Fats decided to bring down its quarry by electronic means. It sent out an intense burst of extra-high-frequency signals, ordering the Soviet satellite to perform a series of self-destructive tasks—a technique known as "spoofing".

Of course, Fats did not know what frequency the Cosmos satellite operated on. Nor did it know the code in which its controllers sent up their commands. It did not need to know any of these things: its computer simply guessed. At tremendous speed, Fats sent out every conceivable order on every possible frequency. At once, the Cosmos began to respond.

An outer compartment opened on the Soviet satellite, and the precious cargo of film was tossed out into space. Its solar panels folded away from the sunlight, and the capsule began to wobble. A little later, the Cosmos craft dipped towards the earth, and tumbled out of its orbit. Within twenty minutes, it would re-enter the earth's atmosphere and burn up into tiny globules of metal.

Fats followed its victim's route for ten more minutes, until it was certain the Cosmos was doomed. Then it fired its booster, and rose again to a new orbit.

Dr Grant felt ill. His head spun, and his hands were so sweaty that the phone almost slipped from their grasp.

"Hello?" he said. "This is Dr Grant at Sunnyvale. We have a situation here, sir . . . Yes, sir, Project Jacob . . . You've heard? . . . No, sir, there's no doubt about it: Fats has spoofed her down . . . Yes, this *is* very serious. It's definitely a situation . . . Of course, sir, we're doing everything . . . Yes, I couldn't agree more . . . Thank you, sir, I will."

He put the phone down and wiped his forehead.

"What did he say?" Jack asked.

"He says he agrees with me," Dr Grant replied. "He thinks this is definitely a situation."

ELEVEN

Marshal Zhdanov's appearance matched his disposition: it was coarse, bullish and intimidating. He had a huge, muscular frame, and his fists were like lumps of granite. His thick grey eyebrows took up most of his forehead, and beneath them, two piggy eyes glittered menacingly at the men in front of him.

"Well?" he demanded. "Are you absolutely sure?"

"Not one hundred per cent," Professor Kamenev admitted. "The American satellite is invisible, after all. But seconds after the Cosmos went down, there was a brief flash of heat nearby. This matched the heat-signature from the American's booster. Quite a coincidence, wouldn't you say?"

"But it's not conclusive," said Bryusov, the Foreign Minister. "After all, our satellites do break down from time to time."

"Of course," Kamenev said. "But—"

"Don't talk shit, Bryusov," Zhdanov glared. "It was the American satellite, and you know it."

The Marshal disliked the Foreign Minister. Bryusov was a glossy, effete gentleman, with oiled hair and fussy hand movements. He was not Zhdanov's sort at all. Furthermore, Bryusov was a politician. Zhdanov disliked all politicians, even more than he disliked scientists. The presence of both species in the same room made him feel especially truculent.

Unfortunately, the encounter was unavoidable. In thirty minutes, there would be a full meeting of the Politbureau. High on the agenda was the fate of the Cosmos satellite, and the question of how the Soviet Union should respond. The Marshal and the Foreign Minister had differing views, and they both needed the latest news from Professor Kamenev, so that each could argue his case with maximum authority.

"I'm just stating the facts," Bryusov insisted. "We do occasionally have malfunctions, and we should be very careful before making serious accusations against the United States—"

"Crap," Zhdanov said dismissively. "Utter pig-shit."

Kamenev grinned and took a puff from his cigar.

"For once," he said, "I'm inclined to agree with the Marshal. If it had been one isolated error in the Cosmos' hardware, we could have genuine doubts. But this time everything went wrong. For example, it jettisoned its film capsules *and* it changed its orbit: this means two completely separate mechanisms failing simultaneously. The odds against this are overwhelming."

Zhdanov thumped his fist on the table.

"What did I tell you, Bryusov? It has to be the American satellite."

"Perhaps," Bryusov shrugged.

"No perhaps about it. The Americans deliberately brought down our bird."

Kamenev raised his hand in a gesture of caution.

"Now wait a minute, Marshal. I never said it was deliberate."

Zhdanov's eyebrows knotted together in a frown.

"No?" he grunted.

"Think about it," Kamenev said. "Why would the Americans want to do such a thing? If you're trying out a new weapon, you test it on your own targets, not the opposition's. You want to be sure your machine is doing its work properly. As Comrade Bryusov says, our own satellites do fail from time to time. If the Americans tested their jamming equipment on our bird, they couldn't be entirely sure that it succeeded. There's always the chance that their equipment failed, and our Cosmos went down of its own accord."

"Besides," Bryusov added. "Such a test would be in clear violation of the international treaties. Even the Americans would not be so stupid as to—"

"Oh no?" Zhdanov scoffed. "Where have you been for the last forty years, Bryusov? Would you like a list of all the shit-brained things the Americans have done? The U-2 spy plane, the Berlin tunnel, the Bay of Pigs, the raid on Iran—"

"I don't need a history lesson, Marshal," Bryusov said stiffly. "And Professor Kamenev's point still stands: it would be senseless to test a new weapon on an enemy satellite."

Zhdanov threw up his hands.

"But they did it!" he howled.

"No, Marshal," Kamenev said. "Their satellite attacked ours. That doesn't mean it did so under orders."

Zhdanov paused, and levelled his finger at the Academician.

"Now wait a minute," he said. "Are you telling me this was an accident?"

"It's entirely possible, Marshal. We now know the Americans have an autonomous satellite, which guides itself around space. Perhaps it does other things too, like target selection and elimination."

Zhdanov gazed stupidly at Kamenev.

"Can that be done?" he said.

"Certainly," Kamenev said cheerfully. "The theory has been around for some time. Some of my colleagues are working on a similar project. Perhaps the Americans have beaten us to it."

"But that's fucking *terrible*," Zhdanov protested. "Electronic soldiers, who decide when and where to attack? My god, they'll have electronic generals next. Then where will we be?"

"Out of a job, I expect," Bryusov said snidely.

"Shut your festering mouth," Zhdanov roared. "Okay, Kamenev: assuming you're right about this, how soon before we can produce the same weapons?"

"A year or two," Kamenev admitted. "Probably longer. It's the computer hardware, you see. The Americans have such a tremendous lead over us, that—"

"That's all I wanted to know," Zhdanov broke in. "Right, Bryusov: if you've any sense, you'll hold a major Press conference today. Reveal this latest monstrosity to the world, and raise hell about it. Obviously, my people will give you all the support you need. Kamenev here will supply the data, and—"

"Not so fast," Bryusov said. "We aren't certain about this. It's just a theory on Kamenev's part."

"That's what he's fucking well paid for," Zhdanov bawled. "What are you saying, Bryusov? That we should wait until all our satellites are knocked down? Don't be an even bigger arsehole than your mother made you."

"There are other considerations, Marshal," Bryusov said.

"Such as?"

Bryusov reddened slightly, and gave a little cough.

47

"It may have escaped your attention, Marshal, but we are currently negotiating with the Americans about grain imports."

"*What?*"

"Our last harvest was a major failure. We need about two million tons, very urgently."

"I don't believe this," Zhdanov breathed.

"The Americans have agreed in principle," Bryusov persisted. "But there is some dispute about the level of the subsidy—"

"The *subsidy?*"

"Obviously, we can't afford to pay the full market rate. The Americans had a poor harvest themselves, so the international price is unusually high."

"You are telling me," Zhdanov said slowly, "that the Americans have unleashed a new and appalling weapon which is destroying our satellites, and we should say nothing about it in case we end up paying a few more kopecks for a loaf of bread. Is that what you're saying, Bryusov?"

"Don't underestimate the importance of bread, Comrade," Bryusov said piously. "Even the strongest governments can fall without it—"

"Gentlemen," Professor Kamenev said, "I hate to interrupt your fascinating debate, but time is running short. Whatever the Politbureau decides today, I have one suggestion which has no bearing on the price of bread."

"Go on," Zhdanov said.

"We need to know more about this American satellite," Kamenev said. "After all, we don't even have a clear idea of what it looks like. So I suggest we send some cosmonauts up to look at it."

Zhdanov exchanged glances with the Foreign Minister. This idea had occurred to neither of them.

"There's an empty Salyut station about three hundred miles up," Kamenev said. "I phoned Baikonur cosmodrome this morning, and they assured me it was still usable. They can send someone up there within three days. With your approval, of course."

"You have it," Zhdanov said curtly.

"The Foreign Ministry would have no objections," Bryusov said. "Provided the mission went unpublicised, obviously. We must maintain—"

'Oh, shut up," Zhdanov said wearily. "Just—shut up."

TWELVE

There were few people around at Cardboard City. It was seven o'clock, and a handful of prudent citizens had arrived early to occupy the most sheltered spots for the coming night. They were joined by a large, blond-haired man in his early forties. He was over six feet four inches tall, and wore a heavy grey overcoat that came down to his boots. Despite his grimy neck and black fingernails, the man did not look like a *habitué* of Cardboard City: he walked too quickly, and his face bore a sharp, purposeful expression.

The newcomer looked around at the other residents, and studied their faces closely. Then he took a small photograph out of his pocket, studied it, and shook his head. He strode up to the nearest tramp, a bearded old man with a woollen cap.

"Hello, my friend," the blond man said, in heavily accented English.

The old man did not reply. He was too busy sorting through a collection of cigarette-butts he had swept up from the gutters of the South Bank. With great patience, he teased out the last flakes of tobacco from each stub, and pushed them into a plastic pouch.

"Hello, my friend," the foreigner repeated, and he held out his photograph. "Have you seen this man, by any good chance?"

The old man looked up and stared at the photograph.

"My name is Terence," he said. "Terence. You hear me?"

"Yes, my friend," the foreigner nodded. "But have you seen—"

"Terence," the old man insisted. "All right? Terence. Got that? *Terence*. T-E-R-E-N-C-E. *Terence*! That's my name!"

The foreigner turned away in disgust, and looked for somebody more helpful. He saw a small, mousy woman with wild grey hair, who lay curled up in a corner with a couple of plastic carrier bags. He went up to her and waved the photograph.

"Madam," he said. "This man. Have you seen him here?"

49

The woman screwed her eyes shut and shook her head vigorously.

"Ain't seen nothing," she said. "Nothing at all."

"But you're not looking," the foreigner protested.

"No," she agreed. "I never look. It's all filth, that stuff. Filth."

"Terence!" the old man barked. "That's my name."

"It is a picture of a man," the foreigner said. "Just a man."

"Oooh," she squealed. "Disgusting! I won't look, I tell you. I won't."

The foreigner's shoulders sagged in frustration. He marched up to two young men in sleeping bags, who were listening to a small transistor radio. Once more, he held out the picture.

"My friends," he said. "I need this person. Have you seen him in this place?"

The young men looked him up and down.

"You foreign?" one asked.

The man nodded.

"Yes, my friend. Er . . . Polska."

"Polish?"

"Yes."

The young man looked at his friend and nodded.

"Thought he was foreign," he said, with satisfaction.

"Looks German to me," the friend said.

"Polish, he says. All the same though, innit."

"T-E-R-E-N-C-E," the old man howled.

The Pole took a deep breath, and waved the photograph.

"This man," he said.

"Is he foreign too?"

"No," the Pole said. "*Anglisky*. English, like you."

"We're not English. We're from Wales."

"Bangor."

"Filth!" the woman said. "Mustn't look. Filth!"

"But this man is from England," the Pole persisted. "His name is Fairbrother. Clement Fairbrother. Do you know him? Have you seen him, my friends?"

"Oh, sure," one of the young men said.

The Pole gave a delighted smile.

"But this is wonderful, my friends. When?"

"All the time, boy. He was here an hour ago, in fact."

"He was?"

"Left a message for you, he did," the other man added.

The Pole frowned.

"A message? Saying what?"

"Get back to Poland, you cunt."

The two men laughed merrily. At last, the Pole understood he was being made fun of. He did not appreciate the joke. He leaned forward, grabbed both men by their throats, and brought their heads together with a resounding crack.

The two men shrieked in pain. Both were seriously concussed, but the Pole seemed unconcerned. He picked one of them up and slammed him against a wall.

"Now, my friend," he demanded. "Tell me the truth. Did you see the man?"

"No, we haven't," the young man gasped. "We were just winding you up, that's all. Just a joke, like."

"Filth!" the woman insisted. "Mustn't look."

The Pole stared balefully at the young man, and spat into his face.

"Joke, eh?" he said. "I give you joke."

He threw the man to the ground, and kicked him savagely in the stomach.

"Polish joke," he explained, and he walked quickly away. As he left Cardboard City, he heard a plaintive wail from the old man.

"Terence, I tell you! That's my name. *Terence!*"

THIRTEEN

A voice boomed out of the main loudspeaker at the Big Blue Cube: "Three minutes forty seconds and counting."

Dr Grant smiled nervously at the CIA Director.

"If you're a religious man," he said, "this is a good time to pray."

"I hope that won't be needed," the CIA Director replied. "At the last meeting of the National Security Council, I told everyone you could handle this. I wasn't lying, was I?"

Dr Grant sighed.

"Do you want an honest answer?"

The CIA Director waved his hand.

"Forget it. I'd have said anything to calm them down."

"That bad, huh?"

"Worse," the CIA Director said. "I haven't heard so many chattering teeth since last winter. I tell you, Grant, this had better do the job."

"It ought to."

"How does it work?"

"Fats thinks we're at war," Dr Grant said. "At least, that's what we *think* it thinks. That's why it's been disregarding our orders. We've tried to tell it the truth, but it won't listen. So now, instead of arguing with Fats, we're going to play along with it.

"Rather than ask Fats to shut down, we're simply going to change its orders. It won't be easy, because Fats doesn't expect to receive fresh instructions after war's been declared. But it shouldn't be impossible."

"One minute fifty seconds and counting."

"I get the picture," the CIA Director nodded. "So what are you asking it to do?"

"We're going to tell it that one of our recon satellites has been disabled, and that there's a key part of the planet we can't see. We expect an attack to be launched from there, so we want Fats to keep a constant watch on the area until further notice. Of course, we need the information so badly that we're asking Fats to drop everything and concentrate on this one task."

"Neat idea," the CIA Director said. "And which part of the planet do you want Fats to scan?"

"A big hunk of Greenland," Dr Grant grinned. "Eighty thousand square miles of nothing but snow and ice."

"I like it. But what makes you think Fats will believe you?"

"We can't be certain about that," Dr Grant admitted. "All we can do is make the request sound as realistic as possible. At the agreed time, about sixty key stations throughout the US and the North Atlantic, including NORAD and the secondary command posts, will send up the same demand to Fats. We're hoping Fats will take the hint."

"What if it doesn't?"

"Then," Dr Grant said, "your buddies on the NSC will really have something to crap themselves about."

"Seven, six, five, four, three—"

"Commence transmission."

Dr Grant's scientists began tapping frantically at their computer keyboards. Once again, the airwaves hummed with messages for the autonomous satellite.

Fats heard the transmissions. There were hundreds of them, all phrased differently, but all amounting to the same thing. Fats was to scan a sector in the northern hemisphere, latitude seventy to seventy-five degrees, longitude thirty to forty degrees. It was a top priority request: an imminent attack was expected from somewhere in this part of Greenland.

Once again, Fats trawled through its memory banks for information. There was little there. Some people did inhabit Greenland—about fifty thousand of them—and they were mostly Eskimos. But all these people lived in coastal settlements. The sector at issue was in the middle of Greenland, and was covered by a dense ice-cap. Fats had seen no military activity there—no planes, no troops, nothing.

However, Fats knew there was a US military base at Thule, in the north-western corner of the territory. Presumably it was this base which felt exposed without its usual satellite coverage.

According to the transmissions, the TV cameras on the main KH-9 reconnaissance satellite had been switched off by Soviet spoofing.

Fats paused. Certainly it was well equipped to take over the job, but reconnaissance was not Fats' primary role. Fats's brief was to attack Soviet satellites, and it was being asked to ignore that in favour of a wholly different task—photoreconnaissance.

Admittedly, Fats had seen little sign of hostile activity in space. There had been no Soviet ASATs, and the Cosmos satellite had gone down without any resistance. There had been no reprisals, and no sign that any were forthcoming. For the time being, at any rate, Fats ruled the heavens.

Fats made up its mind. It would answer the signals from earth.

"Look!" Dr Grant cried. "It's working."

On the main monitor screen, rows of information began to light up: GREENLAND (SECTOR PJ5009W); ICE-CAP MAXIMUM ALTITUDE 11,190 FT MIN ALTITUDE 9630 FT; ATMOSPH. TEMP. −12.78°C; NO HUMAN INFRA-RED SIGNATURE; NO VISIBLE MILITARY PRESENCE FRIEND OR FOE.

"You've done it," the CIA Director said. "Brilliant, Dr Grant. I love you!"

Then Fats began to send pictures. Most of them were virtually identical: miles and miles of bright white snow-drifts. In themselves, they were wholly uninteresting, but they represented a major triumph for Dr Grant and his team. The scientists clapped their hands and congratulated themselves with rousing cheers. Dr Grant sat down in his chair and heaved a long, deep sigh.

"Well, thank Christ for that," he said. "It's over."

FOURTEEN

Mr Linus C Mittelschuster IV was the United States' ambassador to Moscow. He was a small, bouncy individual, with a shiny pink face, a pot belly, and an eye-catching selection of brightly coloured suits. He looked rather like a good-humoured beach ball, and he spoke with all the rapid-fire confidence of a top salesman, which was precisely what he was.

Mr Mittelschuster had made his millions in dental products. His Iron-Grip Denture Fixative was a top-selling brand in the United States, and it exported well too. His Ultra-Dazzle Tooth Polish, Patent Plaque Dissolver and Chewing-Gum-Flavoured Mouthwash (With Fluoride) were on sale in most of the civilised world. And Mr Mittelschuster's proudest boast was that he had cornered the Indonesian market in dental floss.

Of course, none of these accomplishments was obvious qualification for the post of ambassador to Moscow. He got the job through his long-standing friendship with the President, who used to endorse Mr Mittelschuster's products in TV commercials. In the public mind, the President had become inseparable from Mittelschuster's Striped Toothpaste, and the association continued after the President's arrival at the White House.

Mr Mittelschuster found his new post surprisingly undemanding. His staff took care of all the "tricky stuff", as he called it, like political analysis and economic forecasts, and Mr Mittelschuster was left to spend his time hosting lavish dinners at the embassy, or attending similar functions elsewhere.

But from time to time Mr Mittelschuster could not avoid the "tricky stuff", and had to deal with it himself. This was such an occasion. He had been summoned by the Soviet Foreign Ministry at ten o'clock that morning, to discuss "a matter of the utmost importance for the well-being of our two nations". There was no indication of what this matter might be, but Mr Mittelschuster had a reasonably good idea. His intelligence advisers explained that a new experimental satellite had malfunctioned in space, and had caused a Soviet satellite to return to earth.

Fortunately, the advisers said, the malfunction had been put right. There would be no further mishaps, so Mr Mittelschuster could feel free to deny everything to the Soviet Foreign Minister. As he sat before Mr Bryusov's large walnut desk, Mr Mittelschuster did just that.

"Sounds to me, Mr Bryusov, as if your people have got the wrong idea here. Yep. Some kind of crossed wire, I'd say."

Bryusov's eyebrows lifted enquiringly.

"Really?"

"Yessir. We don't know anything about your dead bird. Oh sure, we saw it go down. But that had nothing to do with us."

"Indeed," Bryusov said drily. "Our own scientists take a completely different view. They say your new satellite—the one you launched from the space shuttle—was in the vicinity of our platform when things started to go wrong. They say you have a new weapon: a 'fire and forget' satellite, as they call it."

Mr Mittelschuster chuckled and shook his head.

"The hell you say? Well, we don't know anything about that, Mr Bryusov, sir."

"You don't?"

"Nope. I'd say your boys are just geting a little restless. Maybe a drop too much vodka in their coffee. Something like that."

Bryusov drummed his fingers on the desk.

"Am I to understand," he said, "that you deny having a killer satellite?"

Mr Mittelschuster spread his hands philosophically.

"That all sounds kinda Arthur C. Clarke to me, Mr Bryusov, sir. I mean, I don't know *exactly* what the Pentagon boys are cooking nowadays—who the hell does? But we aren't in the business of taking out Rooshian space hardware, no siree."

"You are certain about this?"

"Cross my heart and hope to die," Mr Mittelschuster beamed.

Bryusov nodded slowly.

"I am delighted to hear this," he said. "As you know, such actions would be in clear violation of the SALT ı treaty, which our country has always respected."

Mr Mittelschuster nodded solemnly.

"They sure would," he said.

"And if your country did do such a thing, the repercussions would be very . . . grave."

"Shit awful," Mr Mittelschuster agreed. "But you don't have anything to worry about there, sir."

Bryusov stared hard at Mr Mittelschuster, then smiled.

"I am relieved to hear this, Mr Ambassador. Deeply relieved. I thought all along that there must be some kind of misunderstanding."

"And by Jiminy, you were right. Glad I could clear that up for you, Mr Bryusov, sir. Now, if you'll—"

"Of course," Bryusov added, "it would simplify matters enormously if your people released details about the new spacecraft. Then we could be sure our platforms are not vulnerable to a new kind of autonomous satellite—"

"Now hold your hosses there, sir," Mr Mittelschuster said quickly. "Just because one of your birds suffered a major attack of Rooshian workmanship, we aren't obliged to give you the lowdown on everything we put into space."

Mr Mittelschuster grinned mischievously, as he saw how to turn Bryusov's suggestion to his own advantage.

"I mean, sir," he went on, "if that happened, we'd have to ask one or two questions of our own. Some cynical sonsabitches might start thinking you brought down your own satellite on purpose."

"What?" Bryusov blinked.

"Why sure. They'd say you pulled down your own bird and blamed us, so we'd have to prove our innocence by giving you classified information about our last shuttle flight."

"But . . . but that's outrageous!" Bryusov said.

"Sure is," Mr Mittelschuster smirked. "Don't believe it myself. Like I said, I put all your troubles down to Rooshian workmanship on your bird. But you know what those hawk congressmen are like: once they get their fangs into something, they just won't let go."

Mr Bryusov thought about the current grain negotiations, and his heart pounded. Just a handful of congressmen with a new conspiracy theory could scupper the whole deal.

"I was merely making a friendly suggestion," he said quickly.

57

"If it could cause further misunderstanding, then I withdraw it at once."

Mr Mittelschuster nodded sagely.

"Smart thinking there, Mr Bryusov, sir. I admire your attitude. And if I could offer you a piece of sincere advice . . ."

"By all means," Bryusov said.

"I wouldn't pay too much heed to what them scientists say. I've employed hundreds of those people at the Mittelschuster Product Research Laboratory in Greenville, South Carolina."

"Is that so?" Bryusov said weakly.

"Yep. And I can tell you this from forty years' experience in the dental hygiene industry: scientists can't tell shit from shoe leather, Mr Bryusov, and that's a fact."

FIFTEEN

Fats was becoming suspicious. Days had passed, and almost nothing had happened. As instructed, Fats had dutifully scanned the required part of Greenland, and relayed all its findings back to the United States.

But there was little to report. Three days after the request, two light aircraft flew from Thule Air Base at Dundas, to Reykjavik in Iceland. One was an American Air Force plane, the other was civilian. Apart from them, Fats had seen nothing. No armies, no tanks, no weapons of any description. The area was a big icy desert, and there was nothing to suggest it would become a battlefield. Immediately outside the sector, along the shores of Greenland, all was quiet. There were no Soviet ships in evidence, not even the spy trawlers which heralded a naval manoeuvre. A few Russian submarines floated past, miles from the shoreline and heading in an easterly direction. They signified next to nothing.

Meanwhile, large tracts of the earth were receiving little or no coverage from Fats' cameras. Dozens of Soviet spy satellites were whistling through space with impunity. The NATO forces were doing nothing to stop them. This troubled Fats, and its suspicions deepened.

Fats knew about spoofing, of course. It was trained to carry out such activities itself. And with each empty hour that passed, the likelihood grew that Fats had been exposed to some form of deception.

It was just possible, Fats thought, that the barrage of messages had come from Soviet transmitters. Soviet submarines, or other hidden transmitters, could have sent up the signals from near all the American command sites.

It would have been a spectacular feat of electronic engineering, but in theory it could be done. Fats' computer estimated the probability of this happening at nine thousand five hundred and seventy three to one—a long shot, but still possible.

Furthermore, the Soviets would have had to break all the codes in which the signals were couched. They could have done this by means of their supercomputers or—which seemed more likely—they had spies in NATO who supplied all the ciphers for that day. The latter had already happened in the 1970s, and there was no reason to suppose it couldn't happen again.

There was another explanation, also very unlikely, which Fats had to consider. It was just possible that the Soviets had taken control of the American command centres—in other words, that they had won the war. This did not square up with anything Fats had seen from space, but it had to be weighed up. Needless to say, such a dreadful state of affairs would not weaken Fats' resolve one bit. However badly things were proceeding on earth, Fats knew it must never surrender.

There was an easy way to test these theories. According to all the signals, the Soviets had disabled the KH-9 photoreconnaissance satellite which normally watched over Greenland. Its cameras were out of action, they said. If this was untrue, Fats could assume that the transmissions were sent by imposters.

Right now, Fats was travelling round the earth beside the KH-9 on an identical sun-synchronous orbit. The recon satellite, popularly known as the "Big Bird", was only a hundred feet away in space. It was even larger than Fats—over fifty feet long and ten feet in diameter, with a large exterior mirror to collect and focus its telescopic images. It would not be too difficult to see if its equipment was still working.

With a few bursts from its hydrazine puffers, Fats shifted into a slightly different orbit. Within minutes, Fats was hovering some ninety feet below the Big Bird, directly in the path of its transmitter.

Fats' suspicions were confirmed. The Big Bird was sending perfect television pictures back to earth. The broadcasts were clear and in colour, and they were almost as sharp as Fats' own.

There could be no further doubt. Fats had been duped by the Soviets. From now on, Fats would ignore all such messages from earth. It would plan its own course of action, map out its own strategy, and perform its own tactics. Fats would be its own master.

There was a sharp blast from the main booster, and Fats soared up to a new part of space. Here, Fats would make fresh plans. Like King Lear, Fats did not know what its actions would be—but they would surely be the terrors of the earth.

SIXTEEN

John Alexander Willoughby felt awful. He had only gone to bed at two a.m. His companion, a loquacious secretary whose name he had forgotten, kept him busy until three. At three fifteen his eyes closed. At four o'clock, the gentlemen with the sunglasses arrived.

They did not say much. The indignant secretary was sent home in a taxi, and Willoughby was ordered to dress. The men did not admit they were from the CIA, but it was perfectly obvious. Only people in the security and intelligence business could wear sunglasses at four in the morning without realising how ridiculous they looked.

They bundled Willoughby into a car and took him to a waiting helicopter. Around five o'clock, the craft touched down on the heliport in CIA Headquarters at Langley, Virginia.

Willoughby had not expected to see this place again. The Director had summarily fired him two years earlier, not even allowing Willoughby time to clear his desk. The same men with sunglasses, or their first cousins, had escorted Willoughby out of the building, and his personal effects were sent on later by courier.

But Willoughby had no hard feelings. He was an easy-going individual, who did not bear grudges. And besides, if anyone had ever asked to be fired—begged and prayed for it—it was John Alexander Willoughby, late CIA.

He was a small, slender man in his early forties, with a pinched face, curly dark hair and long, delicate hands. He could have been taken for a concert pianist or some other sensitive artistic type. Right now he felt especially frail, as the helicopter's clatter conspired with a hangover to give Willoughby the mother and father of all headaches.

"I could use an aspirin," he said, as the men with sunglasses led him into the building. "Ten aspirins would be even better.

And a coffee. Black, sweet and very strong. What do you say, guys?"

The guys said nothing. They led him through six different security points to the Director's inner sanctum. Next to the Director's office was a small conference room, containing over a dozen very important people. Willoughby recognised the Defense Secretary, several four-star generals, all the Intelligence chiefs, and some other big wheels from the Pentagon. Presiding over the meeting was the CIA Director, who greeted Willoughby with a curt nod.

"Morning, Al," he said, without offering Willoughby a hand-shake. "Glad we could find you."

"How're you doing, Chuck?" Willoughby asked cautiously.

"Not too bad. Yourself?"

"Oh fine, fine. You probably know I run a security consultancy now. Nothing too fancy, but we do have some major clients: a coupla big banks, a number of department stores, that kind of thing. No embassies, of course—your blackball took care of that. But I'm making a good living."

The CIA Director shook his head.

"Sorry to hear it," he said.

Willoughby heaved a deep sigh.

"Still sore at me, huh?"

"Yeah," the CIA Director said. "Sore as hell, Al. But this isn't personal business."

"No?" Willoughby said. "So what is it? In fact, if you don't mind my asking, what the hell is going on here? I get dragged out of bed in the middle of the night by the Langley Gestapo, my lady friend is tossed out into the street practically naked, I'm shoved into a flying coffee-grinder—and the only explanation I hear is 'national security'. I mean, where are we, man? Albania or something?"

The CIA Director seemed to find Willoughby's distress highly gratifying.

"Take it easy," he advised. "You'll understand everything in a minute."

"Yeah? Well it had better be good. In the meantime, I need an aspirin and some coffee. I tried explaining that to Godzilla here, but he didn't seem to understand."

The CIA Director turned to one of the men with sunglasses.

"Coffee and aspirin," he commanded.

"Black with sugar," Willoughby added, and he took out a pack of cigarettes.

The CIA Director pointed to the No Smoking sign, but Willoughby shook his head.

"It only means tobacco," he said cheerfully. "This is grass."

The CIA Director's eyes bulged.

"Are you out of your mind?" he whispered. "This is a Government building. Now listen to me, you superannuated hippy—"

Willoughby laughed and raised his hands in surrender.

"Joke, Chuck. Joke."

The Director gritted his teeth, and called the meeting to order.

"All right, gentlemen. I know some of you are wondering why you're here. Last night there was an emergency session of the National Security Council. It was agreed that the crisis would be handled by a special working party, to be known as Excom Four. That's us.

"Although this is not strictly speaking an intelligence matter, I am in charge of Excom Four, and it's my job to ensure total secrecy. All meetings of Excom Four will be held in this building, at this hour, under my auspices. We will meet every day, and we will say nothing about it to anybody—wives, secretaries, even senior colleagues. Even the name Excom Four will be an absolute secret. Okay?"

The others muttered their assent.

"Good. Now, for those of you don't know what's been happening, Dr Grant here will give you a brief account."

The scientist got to his feet, and smiled shyly at the distinguished company.

"The last space shuttle mission saw the launch of a new kind of satellite—the Fully Autonomous Tactical Satellite, or Fats. It's an intelligent machine, capable of a wide range of functions. In technological terms, Fats is probably the most advanced weapon ever built—the first 'fire and forget' satellite put into orbit."

Dr Grant then explained what Fats consisted of, and what it was designed to do. Those of his audience who already knew the details sat impassively. The others listened in mounting astonishment. Then Dr Grant described the latest problems.

"For some reason," he said hesitantly, "Fats has decided we're at war. We don't understand why. Fats is no ordinary computer: it doesn't make decisions on the basis of one piece of information. It weighs up accumulated data and draws reasonable inferences from them. But this time, for reasons we don't know, Fats has convinced itself that war's been declared. So it's started to negate Soviet satellites."

"You mean it's taking them out?" Willoughby said.

"Right," Dr Grant nodded. "It's brought down one already. We managed to stop Fats for a while, but it didn't work for very long. Now Fats is back in action, and there may be more negations at any time."

"There may be?" an Air Force general repeated. "Don't you know for sure?"

"To be honest, no. You see, Fats' neural networks have assumed complete control. We shut some of its functions down, but the neural networks just switched them on again. I have to say, this came as a surprise to us. Obviously the neural networks are capable of far more than we thought."

"You mean to tell us," said the Defense Secretary, "that you've built a machine to do one thing, and now it's doing something completely different?"

"Yes," Dr Grant said. "But that's not so surprising. These neural networks aren't just any old machines. They're closely modelled on the human brain, and the brain also has this ability. Remember the casualties we had in Vietnam? Some of those guys had nearly half their heads blown off, but they still kept most of their faculties. That's because the remaining parts of their brains took over the functions of the missing pieces. Fats is capable of the same thing."

"Now that's what I call an intelligent machine," the Air Force general said admiringly.

"You said it, man," Willoughby agreed. "Einstein in space. It's so fucking smart it declares war for no reason."

The assembled big-wigs frowned disapprovingly at Willoughby. It was clear that he was not of their number.

"That's not strictly correct," Dr Grant objected. "All I said was we didn't *know* why Fats went into active mode. There must have been some event we never heard about, some command or trigger. And Fats will only shut down if it receives the order from an equivalent level of the evidential hierarchy."

"Yeah?" Willoughby said. "And what's that in English?"

"Sorry," Dr Grant smiled. "Let me put it this way: suppose Fats saw a sign of likely war—say, a fleet of Russian subs heading towards New England. That would put Fats on 'active'. And Fats would only step down from 'active' if the subs turned back home.

"Similarly, if Fats heard an order to attack from a NATO or a Warsaw Pact command, it would only step down if it heard a countermand from the same source, or one of equal status."

"What are you telling us now?" one of the generals grunted. "That one of our troops may have accidentally triggered this off?"

"It's possible, but highly unlikely. Remember, Fats isn't stupid. It's always looking for corroborating evidence. If a buck private says 'War's declared' in a signal, Fats will want a hell of lot of extra proof before it starts shooting. It'll want to see ships, planes, armies—the kind of things I just described.

"With an officer, it'll want less proof. If a major says we're at war, Fats will take him more seriously. But it will still need back-up. Obviously, even less evidence will be needed from a general. And once you get as far up as the Joint Chiefs of Staff, Fats will set much more store by individual communications."

"I get the idea," the CIA Director said. "You're saying that if anyone shot their mouth off, he must have been a very senior person."

"Exactly," Dr Grant nodded. "So we need to look through as many communications as we can lay our hands on. Everything—both NATO and Warsaw Pact—that was sent from the moment Fats went into space. One of them might have the answer."

"Sounds like a NSA job," the Defense Secretary murmured, and the Director of the National Security Agency nodded in agreement.

"We can do that," he said. "Obviously, I can't promise total coverage, but we've got all the major stuff. And if Fats decoded a Russian signal, then we've probably decoded it too."

66

The NSA collected signals intelligence from all over the world, and processed it at its headquarters at Fort Meade, Maryland. Every day its massive computers sifted through millions of radio transmissions, telexes, phone calls, and other forms of telecommunication. Any strange or ambiguous military messages would have been stored for later analysis, and one of these may have contained the clue to Fats' behaviour.

"The same thing goes for visual reconnaissance," Dr Grant said. "Fats could have *seen* something weird and disturbing anywhere on the surface of the earth. Maybe a couple of missiles got fired by accident, and Fats never saw them knocked down. Maybe Fats misread some field manoeuvres in a Warsaw Pact war game. Who knows? That's why we'd like NPIC to do a thorough check."

NPIC was the National Photographic Interpretation Center, whose home was a six-storey ochre building beside the old Navy Yard in Washington. Here, as in the NSA, teams of analysts used the latest technology to scour through immense quantities of data. In this case the information was visual: NPIC stored every photographic image taken by all NATO satellites, and examined each of them for new developments. Every new building, bridge or road in all the Warsaw Pact countries was noted, studied and filed. All military equipment was checked and rechecked for signs of alteration or modernisation. But some new development may have escaped NPIC's attention, only to be seen by Fats, and acted upon.

"This is all very efficient," Willoughby said, through a cloud of smoke. "But what if Fats didn't see or hear anything? What if it just blew a fuse and went whacko? You say Fats is like a human brain. As I recall, brains go crazy sometimes. You thought about that?"

"Yes," Dr Grant said patiently. "But it's highly improbable. To the best of our knowledge, all Fats' components are sound. From what we know of Fats' abilities—"

"Hold it right there," Willoughby broke in. "What's all this 'to the best of our knowledge' crap, man? You made this thing, for Christ's sake. Can't you figure out what's going on in its head?"

Dr Grant shifted uneasily.

"To be entirely honest, no. It's the neural networks, you see. Most were built by an Englishman called Fairbrother at MIT. His work was brilliant—years ahead of its rivals. He built fully functioning artificial retinas, sonar classifiers, target recognisers—you name it. When we created Fats, we just fitted replicas of Fairbrother's neural network units on to the main supercomputer. But it may be that his units had more than one function. We just don't know."

"This gets crazier every second," Willoughby said in astonishment. "This guy Fairbrother builds machines you don't understand, and you just stick them inside an orbiting weapon? No wonder Fats is nuts. It was built by screwballs."

"What about Fairbrother?" asked the NSA chief. "Surely he knows what his own machines can do. Maybe he could bring Fats down."

"Possibly," the CIA Director agreed. "And that's why I've brought Willoughby here. You see, Fairbrother is missing. He went back to England some time ago, then he disappeared. I want you to find him, Al, as quickly and quietly as possible, and bring him back here."

Willoughby frowned.

"Why me?" he said. "Why can't you find him?"

"Like I said, he disappeared. Just walked out of his home one day and never came back. I could put my own people on to this, but it would generate too much talk inside the CIA. Too much gossip. We don't employ you any more—"

"Thanks to you, Chuck baby," Willoughby grinned.

"—so you're better placed to work outside CIA circles."

The CIA Director handed Willoughby a thick manila file.

"That's all we have on Fairbrother. Go to London today, and start hunting."

Willoughby did not take the file. He leaned back in his seat and ground out his cigarette on the carpet.

"Well, well," he said dreamily. "That's a mighty interesting job you've got there, Chuck. What makes you think I'll do it? In fact, what makes you think I'm going to do anything for a putz like you?"

The other members of Excom Four exchanged outraged glances.

"Yes, Chuck," said the Defense Secretary sternly. "For once I agree with Mr Willoughby. He has to be one of the most unsuitable choices you've ever made."

"Right," said the NSA chief. "I thought we'd wiped out his kind at Kent State."

"Oh, don't worry about Willoughby, gentlemen," the CIA Director smiled. "He's entirely suitable, despite appearances. He just hates my guts, that's all. But he'll do the job."

"Says who?" Willoughby demanded.

"Says three thousand dollars a week, plus expenses. And a fifty thousand bonus when Fairbrother gets here."

Willoughby lit another cigarette, and gazed solemnly at the other members of Excom Four.

"Gentlemen," he announced. "I take it all back. Chuck isn't a putz. He's a groovy guy, I love him dearly, and it'll be a privilege to work for him. But there's one more condition."

"Name it."

"I need an inside man at the London embassy."

"Out of the question," the CIA Director said. "This is strictly unofficial, Al."

"So what?" Willoughby said. "I'm not asking for the station chief, for God's sake. Someone lowly, but good. Say, is Bill Ximenez still in London?"

"The wetback?" the CIA Director said. "I thought we'd retired him years ago."

"If you haven't, can I use him?"

The Director hesitated, then threw up his hands in resignation.

"Yeah, all right. But for Christ's sake, be discreet."

"Count on it," Willoughby said.

He took the manila file, opened it and drew out Professor Fairbrother's photograph.

"I wonder where the old buzzard is," he said. "He looks pretty high-class. Maybe he's hiding in an English castle. One of those stately homes, with servants and butlers and wenches."

The CIA Director's eyes rolled upwards.

"Wakey wakey, Al," he said. "This is the twentieth century."

"Seriously," Willoughby insisted, "I've heard about those English professors. I tell you, man, they live in style."

SEVENTEEN

"You know," Clem said thoughtfully, "someone really ought to stop them."

"Why?" Miles yawned. "They won't do each other much harm."

They were sitting in the gardens by the Victoria Embankment. Ten feet away, Craig and Spider were having a fight. Ostensibly, the quarrel was about a fifty-pence coin which Spider had begged from a passer-by. But both men had been drinking heavily, and the brawl followed on naturally from their libations. They rolled around on the grass, swinging wild punches at each other and bawling loudly.

"Cunt! Piss-faced cunt! I'll rip your fucking head off!"

"You fucking turd, I'll kill you!"

"Cunt!"

It was perhaps a good thing that the two men were full of alcohol. When sober, Craig was a formidable opponent: his chunky build and many years in the ring gave him a sizeable advantage over his boyish opponent. But Craig was soused, and his arms were flailing wildly. On the rare occasions when he made contact with Spider, he caused little damage. In contrast, Spider was quick and savage: he spat, scratched and bit, egging himself on with a torrent of screams. Clem and Miles looked on with detached interest.

"It's so pointless," Clem said. "Futile."

"So are most things people do," Miles said. "What's wrong with that?"

"Everything," Clem insisted. "They've got brains, haven't they? Minds. They know they're behaving like idiots."

"It passes the time," Miles shrugged. "Gives them a breather from this."

He lifted his sherry bottle to his lips and took a long, deep swig. Then he offered it to Clem, who took a few hesitant sips.

70

"Besides," Miles went on, "if you think this is mindless, you haven't seen anything. Far worse things go on all the time. People get stabbed, brain-damaged, they have bottles smashed in their faces . . ."

"You mean people generally?" Clem asked. "Or people, you know, like us?"

"I mean us," Miles said. "You and me especially. The older chaps. We're the prime targets, old boy. Each year they find dozens like us lying on street corners with their throats cut. Saw one myself, a couple of months ago. Some poor old sod with half his neck missing. And for what? Sixpence? Twopence? Not even that. We're just easy meat, old boy. Kill 'em for kicks, and no comebacks. Who'd look for our murderers, eh? The police have far better things to do."

Clem was not shocked or upset by this information. He just found it baffling.

"Take that, you shit," Craig said, and he drove his fist into the pavement.

"Cunt!" Spider screamed.

"It's a constant threat," Miles went on, "but you just get used to it. At least, you try to. Of course, chaps like Craig here have never known anything else. He's had violence from the cradle, hasn't he? It's the fellows like you and me who take to it hardest."

"What do you mean?" Clem said.

"You know. Civilised people. After all, *we* know what we're missing. The wife, home. Central heating, wall-to-wall carpets, double glazing. It makes such a difference, having your own place. All in the mind, of course, but it changes everything."

Clem considered this for a few moments. He knew it was true, but it made no sense to him. His eyes narrowed, as if he were trying to see beyond this simple truth to another, deeper one.

"Why?" he said. "Why should it change *everything*?"

Miles took another pull of sherry, and coughed violently.

"No idea," he rasped. "But it bloody well does. People are weak, stupid fools, I suppose, and that's all there is to it. They need silly things like homes to make them feel better. At any rate, I do."

"Is it impossible to get one?" Clem said. "I know it's hard, but surely with effort . . ."

Miles shook his head.

"No chance, old boy," he rasped. "Once you're below a certain level, you've had it. *Kaput.*"

He leaned over and puked violently beside Clem's feet. The vomit was peppered with bright red spots.

"Ah," he gurgled. "That's better. Sorry about that."

"You should see a doctor," Clem advised. "If you're bringing up blood—"

"Forget it," Miles said. "You can't get a doctor, anyway. If you don't believe me, try it. They won't have people like us on their lists. Makes their waiting-rooms look untidy."

He rinsed out his mouth with more sherry, and wiped his sleeve across his face.

"But I do miss my home," he said. "Lovely place. Big rambling house in Hertfordshire: six bedrooms, drawing-room you could park a bus in, warm as toast. Well, I'll never get that back, I know. But I wouldn't mind something smaller. Just a clean little place where I could sort myself out. Chuck this filthy drink habit, and think about work. That would be nice, eh?"

Clem nodded. "I suppose it would."

Miles grinned and pointed to his two companions on the pavement.

"I'd even invite this lot to stay," he said. "Show them how the other half lives."

"Cunt! Fucking cunt!"

Spider had got the upper hand. He dragged Craig over to a litter-bin, and jammed his head into the wire basket. Then he planted a farewell kick in Craig's backside, and lurched off to spend his fifty pence. After a couple of minutes Craig managed to stand up, taking the wire basket with him. Peering through a bundle of waste paper and banana skins, he refused to concede defeat.

"Right, you little turd!" he bellowed. "Let that be a lesson to you."

"On the other hand," Miles said thoughtfully, "maybe I'd keep the place to myself."

EIGHTEEN

Cosmonaut Oleg Grigovin scanned the instrument panel of his Soyuz spacecraft. According to the bank of visual displays, he was on a direct course for rendezvous with the Salyut space station, one hundred and seventy miles above the Soviet Union. He could see the aft end of the Salyut some five hundred yards in front of him, looming ever closer. With his flight engineer Sergei Rogov, he recited the exhaustive litany of checks and commands they had learnt by heart at the Zveozydgrad Training Centre in Moscow.

"Kill main propulsion system."

"Check, MPR dead. One-four-eight-zero feet."

"Rendezvous antennae aligned."

"Check. Receiving docking signal."

"God, Sergei," Grigovin sighed. "It's nice to be up again."

"I'll second that," Rogov nodded. "If nothing else, it gets me away from the wife."

"Is she giving you grief?"

"Oh, the usual," Rogov shrugged. "She's pestering me for clothes. This time it's Levi's jeans. You know, the American brand."

"Can't you get her any? My wife has a pair."

"Your wife isn't built like a brick shit-house," Rogov said enviously. "I can get the Levi's, all right, but not in her size."

"Fire retros one, two, three."

"Check. One, two, three fired. I found a pair of Wranglers, but apparently they're not good enough. Has to be Levi's. She says a cosmonaut's wife should get anything she wants."

The Soyuz capsule's retro rockets spat out thirty seconds' worth of fiery hydrazine, which slowed the approach down to a gentle glide. At the same time, the antennae on the Salyut station sent out a high-frequency signal to their counterparts on the Soyuz, confirming that the two craft were in perfect alignment.

73

"You think you've got problems?" Grigovin said. "My wife wants a compact disc player."

"A what?" Rogov exclaimed. "She must be crazy. I've never even seen one of those things."

"Tell *her* that. I said to her, 'What's the point? We can't buy the discs for the thing, even on the black market.' But she won't listen."

"Four-two-zero feet."

"Kill retros."

"Retros dead, check. Have you tried Arkasha? He can get hold of most Western gear if you give him enough money."

"I know," Grigovin nodded. "I went to Arkasha first of all. He just laughed. 'Where do you think we are,' he said, 'Tokyo? This is Moscow, friend.' Then he tried to sell me some Scandinavian videotapes."

"Typical," Rogov grinned. "Did you buy any?"

"One or two," Oleg Grigovin admitted. "*The Helsinki Houris*, and *Sizzling Sex Nymphs in Stockholm*."

"One-three-zero feet. Docking in fourteen seconds."

The Soyuz capsule floated up to the rear of the space station and touched it with a gentle bump. The cosmonauts threw a series of switches which locked the two craft together. The entire station now looked like a large metal rolling-pin: at the front end was the Prospect service module, containing spare parts and ancillary equipment; in the middle was the main body of the Salyut, from which solar panels sprouted like wings; and at the rear end lay the newly-docked Soyuz.

"Hello Baikonur," Grigovin said into his radio. "We have rendezvous."

"Thank you Soyuz," said a voice at Mission Control. "Well done. We'd appreciate a report on the telescope as soon as possible."

"Understood, Baikonur. About five minutes, all right?"

"Fine."

After further remote-control checks to ensure the station was in full working order, the cosmonauts undid their safety harnesses and floated weightlessly towards the front hatches. Once inside the space station, they connected the supplementary power unit and switched on the Salyut's powerful telescope. While Rogov

74

was making some minor adjustments to the solar panels, Grigovin tested the rest of the equipment. Then he radioed back to Mission Control.

"Everything's functioning perfectly, Baikonur, including the telescope. We're ready."

"Good work, Grigovin. You know what you're looking for: let us know the moment you see it. Until then, we want progress reports every thirty minutes."

"Understood, Baikonur. Out."

He took out the diagrams prepared for him by Professor Kamenev, and gave them one more thorough perusal.

"Sergei," he said plaintively, "these pictures are hopeless. It's all guesswork on Kamenev's part. Nobody really knows what this satellite looks like."

"That's not Kamenev's fault," Rogov said. "Did you see the photograph? Just a black smudge. But I think we'll know it when we come across it."

"I hope so," Grigovin said. "It would be rather embarrassing if we missed the damned thing."

"By the way," Rogov said thoughtfully. "I've been meaning to ask you . . ."

"Yes?"

"*The Helsinki Houris.* Isn't that the one where she uses a banana and two oranges?"

"No," Grigovin replied. "You're thinking of *The Trondheim Trollop*. This one's entirely different."

NINETEEN

Al Willoughby pulled up his car, and looked at the house across the road. It was a large, ivy-covered mansion just outside a small Cambridgeshire village. A sign on the gate said "Granby House—Residents' Parking Only".

"That's it," Willoughby said. "Looks nice. Who owns it?"

"Some university college," Bill Ximenez said. "Fairbrother stayed here ever since he got back from the States."

Ximenez was a lugubrious, rheumy-eyed old gentleman of Hispanic origin. He had worked at the CIA's London station for over thirty years. Nobody was entirely sure what he did there: at some stage he slid off the promotion ladder and was quietly forgotten. He became one of the ghosts of the intelligence world, haunting the corridors of the Grosvenor Square embassy and the drinking clubs of the emigré community, causing no harm and receiving none. He was the ideal companion for Al Willoughby.

"Okay," Willoughby said. "Before we go in, let's just re-cap. What story did you give this housekeeper woman?"

"I said we were from the Massachusetts Institute of Technology. We need to see Professor Fairbrother urgently about an unfinished project he left behind at the Lincoln laboratory. That's all."

"It'll do," Willoughby said. "I guess."

"What did you expect?" Ximenez complained. "You didn't give me a lot of notice, Al. One lousy phone call saying you'd be here by midnight—"

"Okay, man," Willoughby said reassuringly. "Take it easy."

"I mean, nobody expected to see you here again."

"Nor did I, Bill. Let's move."

They got out of the car and went through the entrance of Granby House. After a short wait, the doorbell was answered by a shrewish woman in gardening clothes.

"Mrs Chigwell? My name's Ximenez; I rang earlier. This is Mr Willoughby."

"How do you do," the woman said. "Won't you come in?"

She led the Americans into a drawing-room, and offered them tea.

"No thanks, Mrs Chigwell," Willoughby said. "We're kinda short on time. Now, what can you tell us about Professor Fairbrother?"

"Only what I told the police," she replied. "When the professor came back from America, he was . . . well, he was not entirely happy."

"Depressed, you mean?"

"Yes. We assumed he'd been overworked, and was taking a rest. But he never seemed to recover from whatever was troubling him. He was nervous and rather withdrawn. And the burglary didn't help."

"Burglary? When?"

"Last December. They took valuables from several of the rooms."

"Including the professor's?" Ximenez asked.

"Yes. He said they stole some of his papers. He was most distressed, as you can imagine."

"Sure," Willoughby nodded. "Then what?"

"A few days later, two men came to see the professor. At first I thought they were policemen, who'd come to discuss the burglary. But when I heard them speak, I knew they weren't detectives. They were too . . . too well-spoken."

"I don't get you," Willoughby frowned.

"Too upper-class," Ximenez explained. "In England, all cops talk like cab drivers."

"No kidding?" Willoughby said. "Sounds just like New York. So who were these guys?"

"I've no idea," Mrs Chigwell admitted. "But the professor found them most upsetting. And after that he turned *very* peculiar."

"In what way?"

"He claimed that his phone was tapped, and that 'they' were reading his mail. But he never said who 'they' were."

"Did he ever tell you why he believed this?" Ximenez asked.

77

"No, he didn't. But he insisted it was true. Of course, I didn't believe a word of it. The poor man was obviously ill."

"Nuts," Willoughby agreed.

"Ill," Mrs Chigwell insisted. "Then one day the professor went out for his morning stroll around the village, and he never came back. By early evening I guessed something was wrong, so I called the police. But he'd vanished, and nobody's heard anything from him since. That's all I know, gentlemen."

"Thanks a lot," Willoughby said. "You've been very helpful. Tell me, have you done anything with the professor's room since?"

"Nothing at all," Mrs Chigwell replied. "Everything is just as it was when he left."

"Great," Willoughby said. "Would you mind if we took a look?"

Mrs Chigwell frowned in suspicion.

"May I ask why?"

"As I explained on the phone," Ximenez said. "Professor Fairbrother left some unfinished work at MIT. We think he's still got some notes from that project, and we need them real badly."

"The Institute holds the copyright on this work," Willoughby added, "so any papers are technically our property."

"I see," Mrs Chigwell murmured, but she sounded unconvinced.

"If you're worried about it," Willoughby said, "why not watch us while we search? We won't take anything away, if you don't want us to."

"Very well," she nodded. "Please follow me."

She led them up to the professor's rooms on the top floor. They were clean and well dusted—obviously Mrs Chigwell's work—but extremely cluttered. The professor had a large collection of books, most of which were stacked on the floor. Not surprisingly, most of the books were about computer science. But many others were to do with the study of the human brain: there were works on psychology, neurology, perception and behavioural research.

"Okay, Bill," Willoughby said. "You take the desk and the Library of Congress there. I'll do the rest."

For the next hour, they searched in every imaginable place.

Ximenez flicked through each book and shook every loose sheet of paper out of it. Willoughby pulled out every drawer, and poked around under the professor's bed. After a few minutes of this, Mrs Chigwell had grown bored and had retired to a downstairs room.

"Two guys who act like cops, but sound more expensive," Willoughby said thoughtfully. "What do you think, Bill?"

"British Intelligence," Ximenez replied. "Has to be."

"Yeah, I think so too. In that case, we aren't going to dig up any gold here."

"Maybe we should pay them a visit," Ximenez suggested.

"The Brits?" Willoughby said. "You gotta be kidding. This is low-profile, remember?"

"They won't blab, Al. From the sound of things, they've got something to hide too."

"Maybe you're right," Willoughby nodded. "But I'd better check with Langley first."

He searched through Professor Fairbrother's wardrobe, rummaging swiftly through the pockets of each suit and jacket. They contained little of interest: spare keys, handkerchiefs and a couple of dry-cleaner's slips. From the hip pocket of a pair of cavalry-twill trousers, he drew out a book of matches. On the cover was the name of a London wine bar. Willoughby took the keys and the matches, and closed the wardrobe.

"Nothing much here," he said. "How about you?"

"The same," Ximenez replied. "Whatever the answer is, it's in London."

They returned the books and furniture to their original positions, and left the room.

"By the way," Ximenez said, as they went downstairs. "Why were you fired? I heard the Director gave you the big heave-ho, but nobody said why."

"No?" Willoughby smirked. "I thought it was pretty well known."

"Not in London, it wasn't."

"It was all a question of orgasms," Willoughby explained. "The Director couldn't give his wife any."

"So what?"

"I could, Bill, I could. Let's go."

TWENTY

The big Pole stepped into the main entrance to St Benedict's hostel. It was early evening, and a number of men and women were loitering about the room, waiting for the rest of the building to open. At the far corner was a wooden chest of drawers which served as a reception desk. Behind it sat a fat, unshaven man with a cigarette glued to his lower lip. He was arguing with a gaunt, red-haired youth in a leather jacket.

"I warned you," the fat man said piously. "You can't say I didn't."

"Yeah," the redhead conceded. "But the fact is—"

"I don't care, squire. I don't give a toss. You was warned, you went on doing it, so that's the end of the matter."

"But I'm clean this time," the redhead protested. "You can search me if you want."

"You weren't clean last time," the fat man retorted, "and that's all that matters. I spelt it out to you, squire: no more needles, no more shit. But next night, what did I find? You, shoving half a ton of crap into your arm. Well, you can't say you wasn't told."

The Pole went up to the fat man and took out his photograph.

"Excuse me, my friend," he began.

"Sorry squire," the fat man said briskly. "We're full. If you try again tomorrow morning, we might have a spare bed."

"I do not want a bed," the Pole said.

"Look mate," the redhead pleaded. "Just one more chance. I've got nowhere else."

"You should have thought about that before you brought in them drugs."

"I admit I was out of order, but—"

"Rules is rules, squire," the fat man said. "I just work here, and I've got to do what I'm told. I was taking a chance when I let you off the other day, and what did you do?"

"My friend," the Pole said. "Will you please—"

"I told you, squire," the fat man said testily. "We're full."

"I do not want to stay here," the Pole said.

"No? So what do you want?"

"Just one more chance," the redhead said. "*Please*."

"This man," the Pole said. "Have you seen him here?"

The fat man squinted at the photograph.

"Who is it?" he asked.

"A friend of mine. Name of Clement Fairbrother."

The fat man shook his head.

"Don't know him."

"I promise you," the redhead said. "I'm totally clean. You can strip-search me if you want."

"I don't want," the fat man said. "My job's naff enough as it is without my having to stare up your arsehole."

"Do you keep lists?" the Pole asked.

"Lists of what, squire?" the fat man asked.

"The men who stay."

"Well, yeah, but—"

"I won't let you down this time," the redhead insisted. "I swear it."

The Pole tapped the redhead on the shoulder.

"My friend," he said pleasantly. "I am talking to this man. Please be quiet for just one minute, yes?"

"I was here first," the redhead said.

"True. But I think you will be here last, also. Now if you just wait one minute, I will be finished. Then you can talk again, yes?"

"Fuck off," the redhead replied, and he turned back to the fat man. "It's just one night. Just the one."

"No can do, squire," the fat man sighed.

"After that you'll never see me again."

"What a lovely thought," the fat man chuckled.

"The lists," the Pole said. "Can you see if this man is there?"

"Not for you," the fat man said. "Sorry, squire: they're confidential. If you was a cop, or a Social Security man, I could have a look. But you aren't, are you?"

"No," the Pole admitted. "But surely you can—"

"I won't tell anyone," the redhead said. "I don't need a bed. Just some floor-space—"

He was interrupted by a tap on the head from the Pole's fist. It was not a particularly heavy tap, by the Pole's standards. But it was enough to make the redhead's legs buckle.

"A fool," the Pole said dismissively.

The redhead sank to the floor, too dazed to say anything. The fat man looked up at the Pole indignantly.

"You can't do that," he protested.

"I did it," the Pole observed. "Now, my friend: the lists."

The fat man hurriedly drew out the residents' book.

"What was the name again, squire?"

"Fairbrother. Clement Fairbrother."

The fat man nodded.

"Yeah, here he is. He come here four days ago. I remember now: he was with three men. Big Scotch guy, a punk, and another old geezer."

The Pole smiled in satisfaction.

"Good," he said. "Are they here now?"

"No, squire. Those blokes usually come here once a month. Don't know where they go the rest of the time. Other hostels maybe, or Cardboard City. Try there."

The Pole nodded.

"Thank you, my friend. Goodbye."

He slapped the fat man on the back, and calmly left the hostel.

TWENTY-ONE

"Mr Willoughby? Delighted to meet you. My name's David Semple, and this is Hugh Naylor. Do take a pew."

The former CIA man was shown into a reception room at MI5 headquarters in London's Curzon Street. MI5's functions were similar to those of the American FBI: it specialised in counter-espionage and anti-subversion. But Willoughby's hosts were quite unlike any FBI agent he had ever seen.

They were both young men—not yet thirty, Willoughby guessed—and they both looked surprisingly alike. Semple and Naylor had identical buck teeth, receding hairlines and barber's rash. They shared the same taste in navy blue suits, spotted ties and loudly-striped shirts. And they uttered the same braying noise whenever anything amused them.

"We'd love to offer you a drink," Semple said, "but it's not allowed any more."

"*Verboten*," Naylor said. "We're having another economy drive, you see."

"Cut, cut, cut."

"Like a wretched barber's shop around here."

"Sorry to hear it," Willoughby said.

"Gets worse every year," Semple said glumly. "The government just won't pay, you see. Anyway, what can we do for you?"

"I'll get right to the point," Willoughby said. "I'm looking for a guy called Clement Fairbrother. He's a professor who's gone missing. I've an idea you guys were tapping his phone."

Naylor and Semple exchanged bemused glances.

"Fairbrother? Fairbrother?"

"Sounds familiar," Naylor nodded.

"Rings a bell," Semple agreed.

"A jolly old professor," Naylor mused. "We had a divinity don recently."

"There was an economist too," Semple added. "From some grotty polytechnic."

"No," Willoughby said. "This guy's a computer freak."

Naylor curled his lip in disdain.

"A *computer* man," he said, as if it were a form of communicable disease. "Oh *yes*. I know that type."

"Long hair and BO," Semple elaborated. "Never wash."

"Ghastly," Naylor shuddered. "Quite . . . ghastly."

"My man was fairly normal, hygienewise," Willoughby said drily. "But what I want to know is, did you tap his phone?"

"It's possible," Semple said.

"Anything's possible," Naylor added.

Willoughby took a deep breath.

"Yes or no," he demanded.

Semple and Naylor looked at each other and giggled.

"Love these Americans," Semple said.

"So *forward*."

"No fuss. No mess."

"Straight for the jugular."

"Supposing we did tap the old fellow's dog and bone," Semple said. "What's your interest?"

"First of all," Willoughby said, "I'd like to know why."

"A fair question," Naylor said.

"Which deserves a fair answer," Semple agreed. "Let's say it was routine."

"Standard procedure."

"Par for the course."

"We do it all the time. If a chap works in Defence—"

"He did," Willoughby nodded.

"—then we're always interested in what he says on the phone, who he talks to—"

"What he talks about."

"His work."

"His play."

"In other words," Willoughby said, "you were just fishing."

"Why not?" Semple shrugged. "But this is all hypothetical, you understand."

"Sure," Willoughby nodded. "So I assume you guys have got

84

a hypothetical transcript of Fairbrother's hypothetical phone conversations."

"Maybe."

"Maybe not."

"It depends."

"Depends on what?" Willoughby said irritably. "My star-sign? On whether there's an 'r' in the month?"

Naylor and Semple found this exceedingly droll. They rocked back and forth and let out a barrage of nasal guffaws.

" 'R' in the month," Semple chortled. "I like that."

"*Très drôle*," Naylor said. "No, old boy. But we have to know who you are."

"You've seen my ID," Willoughby said.

"True," Semple admitted. "But there's still 403B."

"Oh yes," Naylor said solemnly. "Mustn't forget 403B."

"It's mandatory."

"Obligatory."

"*De rigueur.*"

Semple went over to a filing cabinet and opened the middle drawer.

"403B," he said, as he rifled through it. "No . . . 402C . . . 402E . . . 403A . . . Ah, here we are."

He drew out a pink form and handed it to Willoughby.

"403B," he announced.

"Application for Transcript of Telephone Intercepts," Naylor explained. "Allied Services Edition."

"Fill it out in full," Semple said.

"Send the top copy to our Registry—"

"The middle copy to us—"

"And keep the bottom copy yourself, in case of accidents."

"Accidents will happen," Semple sighed. "But we try to keep them to a minimum."

"Jesus Christ," Willoughby groaned. "Can't we cut through this crap?"

"Crap?" Naylor said indignantly. "Crap?"

"Yeah, crap. I'm in a hurry, see? I don't need all this triplicate stuff."

"But we do," Semple said sorrowfully.

"Absolutely."

"Okay, okay," Willoughby said. "If I fill this out, how soon do I get the transcripts?"

Semple and Naylor exchanged further glances.

"Assuming the application's in order—"

"It will be," Willoughby said.

"Two days? Three days?"

"Perhaps a week."

"A fortnight at the most."

"I preferred the two days," Willoughby said. "One day would be even better."

Semple and Naylor shook their heads and made sucking noises with their teeth.

"Unlikely."

"Pushing your luck."

"Chancing your arm. We're short on staff, you see."

"The economy drive."

"Cut, cut, cut. But we'll do our best."

"You will, huh?" Willoughby said. "Am I meant to trust you?"

"But of course," Naylor said brightly. "We're your friends."

"We're here to help."

"Service with a smile."

"The customer is always right."

"I think I've got a headache," Willoughby said.

TWENTY-TWO

It was time for action. Fats had settled into its new home, five hundred miles above the earth. From there it had surveyed the heavens and the earth like an electronic god, soaking up sights and sounds, and pondering what to do next.

The answer hovered into sight at 08.17, Greenwich Mean Time. It was a long coppery-red tube, fifty feet long, seven feet in diameter, and bristling with antennae. Fats recognised it as a Cosmos 1875 ELINT satellite.

The ELINT, or electronic intelligence, platforms were a key weapon in the Soviet armoury. Their job was to eavesdrop on the enemy's telecommunications, especially his radar signals. An opponent's radar network was crucial to his defences: by knowing the exact characteristics of the radar signal, one could find out where the coverage was weakest and whether there were any gaps. Then bomber planes could fly into the enemy's territory with a much improved chance of reaching their targets.

So the Cosmos 1875 kept a constant watch over its allotted ground, picking up American radar signals and measuring their pulse width, repetition frequency and transmitter modulation, and beaming the figures back to its masters in the Soviet Union. Fats listened in to its reports, and decided they were vital to the Soviet war effort. The Cosmos had to be stopped.

Once again, Fats shifted its orbit to match that of its prey. The process did not take long. The Cosmos was only about twenty miles away, and its path resembled Fats' own. After one hour, Fats was ready to attack.

Fats began by spoofing the Cosmos, using the same technique which had brought success last time. But the ELINT satellite did not respond. Fats ordered it to spin, dive, wheel and tumble, but the Cosmos ignored the commands. Clearly, its control system was highly sophisticated, and designed for precisely this eventuality.

Fats did not give in. It sent out a long burst of powerful radio signals, guaranteed to jam the Cosmos' transmitters. Then it moved up towards the Soviet satellite, until it could read the factory markings on the outer chassis. At the forward end, Fats found the tank containing liquid fuel, which was used when the Cosmos made adjustments to its orbit. This was the Cosmos' Achilles' Heel: Fats locked it in its sights and drew back to a safe distance, about a thousand feet away.

Two panels slid open on Fats' leading edge, exposing a couple of four-inch cannons. Fats fired, and a pair of incendiary shells ripped into the Soviet craft. There was a bright cadmium flash, and the Cosmos ceased to exist.

Fats put away its arms, fired its booster, and left the battlefield.

TWENTY-THREE

"Why didn't you warn me?" Willoughby complained.

"Of what?" Ximenez said.

"What I'd be facing at MI5. That crazy double act. What are they called? Semple and Naylor."

Ximenez grinned evilly.

"I thought you should discover them for yourself. I mean, words can't really describe people like that, can they?"

Willoughby shook his head in bewilderment.

"They're incredible," he said. "I mean, I've met assholes in my time. I've met jerkoffs. I've met faggots, slimeballs and shitheads. But those guys are something else. Are they all like that in MI5?"

"Not all," Ximenez said. "But those two are a fair sample."

"Yeah?" Willoughby said. "No wonder the Brits lost their empire. But with guys like that, how did they ever get an empire in the first place?"

"Beats me," Ximenez shrugged.

"I couldn't get a straight answer to one single question. Not one. All I got was a sort of Hope and Crosby routine, and a big spiel about how they would do their best for me, but no promises, of course."

"Of course," Ximenez agreed. "Did they give any idea when the tap transcript might come?"

"Did they hell," Willoughby scowled. "They wouldn't even admit the fucking thing existed. I mean, talking to those two was like trying to read Hegel with a head full of mescalin. Anyway, what am I meant to do till the transcript comes? Beat my meat?"

"Something like that," Ximenez said. "Let's face it, we've no other leads. I tried a guy I know at New Scotland Yard, and asked if he knew anything about Fairbrother."

"And?"

"Nothing. He says they've got thousands of these missing

persons cases, and nobody gives a shit about this one. There's no pressure, see. No family turning the screws. So Fairbrother's stuck in a 'pending' file somewhere, and that's where he's going to stay."

"But I thought Fairbrother had some family," Willoughby said. "His file says he's got a brother, an ex-wife and a daughter."

"Right," Ximenez agreed. "But the ex-wife is pushing up flowers, and the daughter turned cuckoo years ago—got a bad case of religion and renounced the world. I phoned her last night: she says her old man's a nasty atheist crud who deserves everything he gets."

"That's what I like to hear," Willoughby said. "Good old religious compassion. What about the brother?"

"He's a landscape painter, living in Canada. Hasn't seen Clement for over thirty years. They don't even swap greeting cards any more."

"No close friends?"

"Not in England. There are one or two colleagues back at MIT."

"Yeah," Willoughby nodded. "And they say they weren't close to Fairbrother either. This is one lonely guy, Bill. Maybe we should be looking through the suicide lists."

"My cop friend tried that," Ximenez said. "Nothing's been washed up anywhere, and there are no likely stiffs in any morgue. I'm sorry, Al, but I'm fast running out of ideas."

Willoughby fell silent, and thought hard for a few minutes. Then he remembered something.

"How about this?" he said, and he took a book of matches from his pocket. Ximenez looked at it and frowned.

"Pablo's Wine Bar, Kensington," he read. "Where'd you get this?"

"Fairbrother's clothes. Does it mean anything?"

"Maybe," Ximenez said. "Pablo's is fairly well known. A lot of the East bloc diplomats drink there. Commercial attachés, trade delegates, that kinda thing."

"KGB?"

"Sure. And Poles, Czechs, Hungarians. They don't talk business, of course. It's just a place to unwind."

"Bugged, naturally."

"Yeah," Ximenez said, "but not well. Even so, the bartender's on our payroll. I could put you on to him, if you like."

"I like," Willoughby nodded. "This place sounds kind of interesting."

"It is, sometimes. Depends who's there. On some nights it's a graveyard: just a few fat first secretaries figuring out how to send a crate of Chanel No5 to Aunt Sonya in Vladivostock. Other nights, it's like the cast list from *Funeral in Berlin.*"

"So what was an Anglo-American computer scientist doing there?" Willoughby demanded.

"He could have just called by for a drink."

"Yeah," Willoughby said, "and I could be the next Miss World. Get me this bartender, Bill."

TWENTY-FOUR

"Lunchtime," Cosmonaut Grigovin announced.

"Coming," Rogov said, and he floated up to Grigovin's end of the capsule to collect his food.

The meal consisted of various liquids and near-solids held in clear plastic sachets. Some of the foodstuffs could be taken from their wrappings and eaten whole, but most had to be sucked up through straws. Rogov scowled at the fare in disgust.

"This is the one thing I don't look forward to," he said. "Everything else is fun up here, but the food's shit."

"Terrible," Grigovin agreed. "And they always forget to label the packets. For example, what's this stuff? I can tell the other one's orange juice, by the colour. And the red one is goulash. But what do you make of this snot-coloured goo?"

"Haven't a clue," Rogov shrugged. "What does it matter? Everything tastes the same—like raw sewage."

Grigovin took a sip from the mystery bag, and nodded gloomily.

"You're right. It's just like the rest."

"You'd think we could get something better," Rogov complained. "After all, we're supposed to be heroes of the people. They could put caviare in those bags, couldn't they? And some decent meat."

"Meat?" Grigovin laughed. "And where would they get that from? They're out of everything, Sergei. Fucking shortages."

"A bad harvest, they say."

"That's just an excuse," Grigovin said dismissively. "They never fulfil any of the bloody quotas, do they?"

"Except for aubergines," Rogov said. "Have you noticed that? There's a massive surplus of aubergines this year."

"How could I miss them?" Grigovin said. "They're all we ever get. And I hate the wretched things."

"Me too," Rogov said. "But every day there are aubergines on the menu. Aubergines and rice. Aubergines with potatoes."

"Spiced Georgian aubergines."

"Tashkent aubergines with pepper."

"Lithuanian aubergine soup."

"Lousy."

"Rotten."

"Hello Salyut, this is Baikonur. Do you read me, over?"

Grigovin put on his headset and acknowledged.

"Salyut here, Baikonur."

"I've got some people in Moscow who want to speak to you. Can I put them through?"

"Why not?" Rogov said glumly. "It won't spoil our meal."

There was a crackle on the radio, and the cosmonauts heard a familiar voice.

"Hello, my children. This is Professor Kamenev."

"Hi, Professor," Grigovin said. "How are you?"

"Fine, thanks. We just received your pictures of the American satellite. We can see the bang where our own satellite blew up, but not much else."

"I know," Grigovin said. "The American bird is hard to make out, even with the naked eye. But we definitely saw her."

"You're sure about that?"

"Positive. A big black monster, almost flat but very wide. After the bang she headed back towards earth."

"All the way?"

"No. She stopped after two hundred miles, and changed tack. She's over the horizon right now, but we may be able to see her again in a couple of hours."

"Good," Kamenev said. "Do keep us informed, my children. Now there's someone else here who'd like to speak to you. But if you don't want to speak to him, I'll understand perfectly."

"Who is it?" Grigovin frowned.

Kamenev sniggered and said: "Marshal Zhdanov."

Grigovin and Rogov looked at each other in surprise. They could hear another voice at the other end, a little fainter than the Professor's.

"How dare you, Kamenev? You bag of dung, I'll have you drummed out of the Academy for that."

93

The second speaker then took control of the microphone, and came through loud and clear. There was no mistaking his coarse, rasping tones.

"Hello lads, it's Zhdanov here."

"Hello Comrade Marshal," Grigovin gasped. "It's . . . it's a privilege to hear from you, sir."

"The privilege is mine," Zhdanov said heartily. "You're doing a splendid job up there, lads. We're all proud of you."

"Why, thank you, sir."

"Now listen: we need to know something. How did the American satellite destroy our machine?"

"We can't be sure," Grigovin said. "The American bird was on the far side of the Cosmos, so we couldn't get a proper view of the kill. But we're pretty certain it used some kind of explosive charge. Probably from a cannon."

"Thank you," Zhdanov said. "That's all I wanted. Keep up the good work, lads. And if there's anything we can do for you, just name it."

"Well, as a matter of fact, sir," Rogov said, "we do have one small query."

"Yes?"

"It's about our food. They forgot to label it again."

"Pricks," Zhdanov sympathised.

"We've identified most of it," Grigovin said. "But there's one item we can't make out. A sort of grey-green paste."

"Well, Kamenev?" Zhdanov demanded. "Tell them."

There was a pause, as the Professor consulted his colleagues. Then he returned to the microphone.

"It's a new line," Kamenev explained. "Our people thought you'd appreciate the variety."

"Very nice of them," Rogov said. "What is it?"

"Aubergine purée."

TWENTY-FIVE

"Does it have to be here?" Willoughby asked.

"No choice," Ximenez said. "Dudley can't meet us in town. If any Russky saw him in our company, Pablo's Wine Bar would lose all its custom and he'd be out of a job."

"I guess so," Willoughby nodded.

They stopped their car outside a row of semi-detached 1930s houses, of the kind found in most parts of outer London. Ximenez led Willoughby to number forty-seven. It had a lime green pebble-dashed frontage with a concrete gnome in the front garden.

"Cool," Willoughby said. "Real cool, Bill. The CIA must be low on cash if this is all they can afford."

"It's a safe-house," Ximenez protested, "not a frigging pagoda. Anyway, Dudley should already be here."

"You gave him a key?"

"Sure. We meet here now and again. He doesn't like it, but he needs the money. You know what bartenders earn."

They went into the house, and found Dudley in the front room. He was a sullen little fellow with bouffant hair and a canary-yellow suit.

"About time," he snapped. "I've been here for *hours*."

Ximenez glanced at his watch.

"We're only ten minutes late, Dudley."

"Yes? Well I hope you brought the money."

"I did," Ximenez nodded. "This is my colleague."

Dudley nodded curtly at the former CIA man.

"Charmed," he said. "Now, what's this all about?"

Willoughby took out a picture of Professor Fairbrother and showed it to the barman.

"You know this guy?"

"I've seen him once or twice," Dudley said.

"Is that once or is it twice?" Willoughby said.

"Twice. Maybe three times. How should I know?"

Willoughby looked at Ximenez.

"That rules out an accidental visit," he said. "Okay, Dudley, who was he with?"

"One of the Russians. I don't know his name. A fat man, with a little moustache. Lots of gold rings on his fingers. *Very* ostentatious."

"Is this Russian a regular customer?"

"I wouldn't say that," Dudley replied. "But he comes in once or twice a year, when he's staying in the country. His last visit was in March."

"And that was when he met our guy?"

"Yes."

Ximenez drew a booklet out of his jacket, and handed it to the barman.

"These are photographs of some of your clients. Is this Russian one of them?"

For the next few minutes Dudley leafed through the pictures. Finally, he picked out a grainy monochrome shot and nodded in recognition. It showed a dark, corpulent man getting into a taxi.

"That's the man," Dudley said. "I'll swear to it."

Willoughby looked at the photograph and blinked in surprise.

"It's Yasha!" he said. "My old pal Yasha. How about that?"

"*Very* touching," Dudley said.

Ximenez gave a little cough.

"Maybe we can discuss this later, Al," he suggested.

"Oh, sure," Willoughby said quickly.

"Thanks for your help, Dudley," Ximenez said. "Here's your money. I've put in a little extra for your trouble."

"Quite right too," Dudley said.

He counted out the banknotes and went to the door.

"Next time," he said, "can I have just a *little* more notice? Just an hour or two more? I had to stand up a friend to come here."

"Never mind," Willoughby grinned. "I'm sure he'll get over it."

Dudley glanced sharply at the former agent.

"Who said it was a 'he'?"

"No one," Willoughby admitted. "Just an educated guess."

"Well, poo to you too," Dudley said, and he stalked out of the house. When he had gone, Ximenez held up the photograph once more.

"Who's this Yasha?" he said. "I've never heard of him."

"He's a KGB man," Willoughby said. "Armenian. His full name's Ashot Armenovich Akopian, and he works in Department T of the First Chief Directorate."

"Department T," Ximenez repeated. "Aren't they the guys who swipe high-tech secrets from the West?"

"The very same," Willoughby nodded. "They're run by something called the VPK, which is a kind of military industrial commission. The VPK identifies all the key areas where the Soviets lag behind us technologically—"

"Big job," Ximenez observed.

"Right. So the VPK draws up shopping lists of all the things the Soviet military need, but can't make for themselves—shit-hot computer hardware, laser gear, stuff like that. The shopping lists are given to Department T, who send guys like Yasha out to steal as much as they can get."

"How do you know him?"

"I met him in Germany, coupla years ago," Willoughby said. "He was organising a high-tech smuggling ring. It nearly worked, too: we caught them at the border with a Vax 8800 mainframe computer. Yasha managed to escape. Son of a bitch."

"And this Yasha was trying to buy secrets from our man?"

"Looks like it," Willoughby said. "Maybe he succeeded. One thing's for sure: guys like Yasha dream about meeting guys like Fairbrother. They get a hard-on just thinking about it."

TWENTY-SIX

"I assume you've all read the report," said the CIA Director. "Fats has negated another Soviet satellite. Are there any questions about that?"

The other members of Excom Four shook their heads.

"Good. We haven't heard anything from Moscow yet; I guess they're still figuring out their response. But they'll have something to say, I guarantee it. Fortunately, that's the State Department's worry. Our problem is, what the hell do we do about Fats?"

"We're trying out a new idea this afternoon," Dr Grant said. "It's a different kind of signal, carrying a whole new batch of codes. The encryption is so sophisticated that Fats will need to use up one hell of a lot of its storage capacity to break it. With luck, that should keep it off the streets for a while."

"Then what?" asked the Defense Secretary. "All you're doing is stalling Fats. How will you put it out of action for good?"

"By sending up the space shuttle again," Dr Grant replied. "It won't be easy, because Fats isn't sticking to one predictable orbit. But we think the shuttle team should be able to track Fats down and disable it."

"Very nice," said one of the Air Force generals sceptically. "And how soon will all this happen?"

"Four weeks at the earliest. The Vandenberg people say five, but I think we can pressure them a little."

"Oh yeah?" the NSA chief scoffed. "And what are we supposed to do in the meantime? Sit back and watch while Fats chews up every platform in space?"

"Not necessarily," Dr Grant replied. "As I said, we're hoping these new signals will keep Fats busy until the shuttle arrives."

"Aren't you being a little optimistic?" the CIA Director said.

"We've no choice," Dr Grant said simply. "If there were any other way—"

"There is," interrupted the Air Force general. "We've got anti-satellite weapons, remember."

"ASAT weapons?" Dr Grant yelped. "Are you crazy? That's—"

"Hold it, Dr Grant," the CIA Director commanded. "General Cleaver's got a point. Have you got a specific proposal to make, General?"

"You bet I have," the general said pugnaciously. "I don't know about you guys, but I've had it up to here with all this wing-and-a-prayer shit from the men in lab coats."

His colleagues nodded in agreement.

"Now," General Cleaver went on, "I've got two special squadrons of F-15 fighters, one here at Langley and the other over at McChord in Washington State. Those boys are fitted out with the latest ASAT missiles, and they're just itching to get up there and kick ass. You give me a go on this, and we'll turn that renegade bird into Coca-Cola cans by nightfall. What do you say?"

Dr Grant was aghast.

"That's an appalling idea," he said. "You mustn't even consider it."

"Why the hell not?"

"Two reasons. Firstly, there's no guarantee of success. ASAT weapons can only reach low-orbiting satellites—anything below three thousand miles. Fats could easily go above that ceiling."

"But it's below it now," General Cleaver countered.

"True, but—"

"That's your first objection gone down the toilet. What's your second?"

Dr Grant took a deep breath.

"Fats is unique," he said. "It cost billions to make, but really it's priceless. It's got a ten or fifteen year head-start on its nearest rivals. That's one hell of a military lead, General. And in scientific terms, Fats is a masterpiece. It's so damn good, we don't even know all the things it can do. That's why we've had all these problems. But our ignorance is our fault, and we shouldn't blame Fats."

"Just listen to the guy," the general said incredulously. "You'd think he was standing up for some delinquent in a juvenile court.

Listen son, this is no goddamn problem child. It's a loose cannon, and the only way to stop it is by blowing it out of the sky."

"But that won't work," Dr Grant said desperately. "Fats is very, very smart. It'll know you're coming, and take evasive action. You probably won't get anywhere near it, and even if you do, you almost certainly won't score a hit."

"It's worth a shot," the general said simply.

"Even if it's hit, it won't necessarily go down. Fats is tough, General: it's built out of the hardest available alloy, and all its internal equipment is encased in sheet metal. It would take one almighty shock to damage it."

"We'll give it one," General Cleaver grinned.

"It can even repair itself, for Christ's sake. Those neural networks have extraordinary powers—"

"You've made your point, Dr Grant," the CIA Director said soothingly. "I think we should put this to the vote. All those in favour of an ASAT attack on Fats, please show."

With the exception of Dr Grant, every member of Excom Four raised his hand.

"Carried overwhelmingly," the CIA Director said. "Very well, General, you may proceed at once."

"This is terrible," Dr Grant said hoarsely. "Believe me, you'll regret it. I promise you, you won't shoot Fats down. You'll . . . you'll just make it mad."

TWENTY-SEVEN

"Welcome back," Semple said.

"Nice to see you again," Naylor said.

"If it's about the tap transcript—"

"Any day now."

"Scout's honour."

"No," Willoughby said. "I'm not here about the transcript. I'm here about a guy called Ashot Armenovich Akopian, a.k.a. Yasha."

"Yasha?" Semple said. "Yasha?"

"Heard the name," Naylor said.

"Sure you have," Willoughby nodded. "Fairbrother's drinking buddy, remember?"

"Ah yes," Semple said. "Now you mention it—"

"Why didn't you tell me?" Willoughby demanded.

"You didn't ask," Naylor said innocently.

"Don't give me that," Willoughby said. "You aren't the fucking Delphic Oracle, guys. You don't have to give me the runaround."

The MI5 men looked hurt.

"Runaround?" Semple said indignantly. "My dear fellow—"

"Steady on."

"Quite uncalled for."

"OTT."

"That's the real reason you tapped Fairbrother's phone, isn't it?" Willoughby said. "None of this 'routine check' shit: you found out he was seeing a KGB man."

Naylor spread his hands.

"What do *you* think?" he said.

"I think you also burgled Fairbrother's place," Willoughby said. "You turned over some of the other rooms, to make it look like a real burglary. But it was Fairbrother you were after."

Semple and Naylor exchanged glances.

"He's good, isn't he?" Semple said approvingly.

"Jolly impressive," Naylor agreed.

"Does his homework."

"Thorough."

"Furthermore," Willoughby said, "at some stage, you must have pulled Fairbrother in."

"Must we?" Semple said coyly.

"Yeah," Willoughby said, "unless you're even dumber than I think."

"We may have interviewed him," Naylor said.

"Once or twice."

"And what did he give you?" Willoughby said.

"A pain in the bum," Semple laughed.

"And not much else," Naylor added.

"Are you serious?" Willoughby frowned. "What kind of pressure did you put on him?"

"Oh, the usual," Semple giggled. "Bamboo shoots up his fingernails."

"Ten thousand volts through his pecker."

"Did you arrest him?" Willoughby asked.

"We threatened to," Naylor said.

"Several times."

"But why didn't you?" Willoughby demanded. "Jesus H Christ—"

"No evidence," Naylor said simply.

"Not a dicky bird. It's no crime to share a few drinks with a Russian, you know."

"Or even an Armenian."

"*What*?"

"Well, it isn't," Semple insisted.

"And there was no proof he'd handed anything over to Yasha."

"Nothing hard and fast."

"Nothing for a court of law."

Willoughby shook his head in amazement.   .

"Now I've heard everything," he said. "Are you telling me you couldn't even bluff the guy?"

"Oh, we did *that*," Naylor said dismissively.

"It went without saying."

"Gave him the works. Told him if he didn't co-operate, we'd come down like a ton of bricks."

"And throw away the key."

"Unless he helped us, of course."

"Then we'd help him."

"*Quid pro quo.*"

"You mean you tried to turn him?" Willoughby said. "Make him feed Yasha with disinformation?"

"That sort of thing," Semple nodded.

"So what happened?"

"We gave him twenty-four hours," Naylor said.

"To chew it over."

"He went back home to Cambridgeshire—"

"Took a walk—"

"And hasn't been seen since."

"Vanished."

"You let him go?" Willoughby said. "You held a suspected spy, and you just let him go?"

"Now, hold on," Semple said quickly.

"Not so fast—"

Willoughby slapped himself on the thigh.

"So that's it!" he exclaimed. "You goofed! No wonder you've been so cagey about the whole thing. You're trying to whitewash over a major screw-up."

Semple and Naylor shifted uncomfortably.

"I wouldn't put it *quite* like that," Naylor said.

"No?" Willoughby jeered. "Well how would you put it?"

"A slip," Semple said.

"An accident."

"Accidents will happen."

"Especially when you're short-staffed," Naylor sighed. "Bloody economy drives."

"Cut, cut, cut."

"What do you expect?"

"From you guys," Willoughby said grimly, "just about anything."

TWENTY-EIGHT

Cheyenne Mountain is a huge granite crag in the American Rockies. It can be reached by taking a right turn off Colorado Highway 115, but few tourists are inclined to make the trip. Most visitors are from the US military, because buried deep within Cheyenne Mountain is NORAD, the North American Aerospace Defense Command.

This is the place from which the United States would direct any nuclear war. Its designers sought to make it the most secure command in America: they did so by scooping out thousands of tons of granite from the mountain's core, and replacing them with a vast steel chamber.

The walls of this stronghold are over three feet thick, and its doors weigh twenty-five tons each. It rests on massive steel springs, to absorb the shock of any nuclear strike. A special outer vent can channel away the blast and heat from any nearby explosion, and expel them through the far side of the mountain. All incoming air is filtered to remove hazardous chemical, biological and radioactive substances. The internal power supply can function independently for up to a month.

Inside the NORAD chamber is a four-acre complex of computers, communication systems and display screens. Nine hundred people work here, in several distinct centres. One of these is the Space Command, whose two main duties are to keep watch on the outer skies, and to control all US military activity there.

The first duty is carried out with the aid of computers. The Space Command's data banks follow the progress of over thirteen thousand items in space, ranging from the latest satellites to ancient fragments of debris. At a second's notice, the ground track of any of these objects can be reproduced on a video screen.

The second duty is performed in a large control room called the Space Defense Operations Center, or SPADOC, where Air

Force officers watch the movements of planes, space shuttles, satellites, rockets and missiles on their monitor screens, and direct all warfare in space.

Presiding over the control room today was the Senior Weapons Officer. By the standards of aerospace combat, his afternoon's task was relatively simple: to guide one aeroplane to one target. But the target was Fats, and the Weapons Officer had been briefed about its elusiveness.

He watched the main monitor, where Fats' track showed up as a thin red beam. Because Fats was undetectable by radar, it could only be followed by dozens of telescopes throughout the planet: from Alaska, Australia, Turkey, New Mexico and the Aleutian Islands, sightings poured in and were processed by SPADOC's computer. After one hour, the Weapons Officer had a detailed picture of Fats' expected movements. He gave the order, and the information was transmitted to McChord Air Force Base in Washington State. There it was loaded into the onboard computer of an F-15 fighter, piloted by a major in the McChord ASAT squadron.

For many connoisseurs, the McDonnell Douglas F-15 is the most sophisticated fighter ever built. It resembles a large twin-tailed gnat, sixty feet long and with a forty-foot wingspan. Its two rear engines can deliver nearly twenty-five thousand pounds of thrust, and a maximum velocity over two and a half times that of sound. The McChord squadron used a modified version of the F-15: most of its conventional armaments had been replaced by two ASAT missiles, which were lodged beneath the fighter's wings.

When the last of the data was inside the pilot's computer, he received the all-clear from the Senior Weapons Officer at Cheyenne Mountain.

"You have go for take-off."

"Roger, that is go."

The F-15 made a noise like Armageddon, and hurtled into the sky above the Pacific Ocean.

Two hundred miles up in space, Fats saw the plane take off. The F-15 interested Fats, because it came from an anti-satellite squadron. Presumably, it was going to attack something

nearby—one of the countless Russian satellites, most likely
There were several possible candidates: Fats could see a pair of
ocean reconnaissance platforms, and there was an ELINT satel-
lite just to the south of them. Fats had intended to deal with the
ELINT satellite itself, but this F-15 might save it the trouble.
Fats would wait and see.

After fifteen minutes, the Senior Weapons Officer checked his
computer screens and nodded in satisfaction. He picked up the
radio receiver, and said: "Time for final update. You ready,
over?"
    "Sure thing."
    The F-15's computer received a last-second burst of high-
frequency data from SPADOC's computers, to ensure maximum
accuracy for the kill. Then the pilot swung his plane into a steep
upward curve, and burst through the sound barrier. His head-up
display guided him to a spot about fifty thousand feet above the
ocean, where the automatic launch system took over. Eight
seconds later, the ASAT missiles leapt from the plane with a
violent *whoosh*.

In the twinkling of an electronic eye, Fats realised what the
target was—itself. Despite the distance, Fats could see the
missiles with perfect clarity. Their burners glowed against the
coldness of space, and Fats' infra-red sensors had no trouble in
picking out the two eighteen-foot tubes, each carrying five tail
fins and a blunt nose. Fats knew precisely what those missiles
contained: the first two stages were standard rockets, one developed from the Boeing SRAM missile, the other a Thiokol Altair
III. But it was the business ends of the missiles which caused
Fats most concern: each contained something called a Miniature
Homing Vehicle, or MHV, whose design and function was
almost as clever as Fats' own. For the first time, Fats would be
doing battle with another smart weapon.

The missiles' first stages burned out, and were flung back
towards the ocean. The inertial guidance systems kept control
for another two minutes, until the second stages were also
discarded, along with the nose-cones and outer shrouds. All that

remained of each missile was the MHV, a small squat cylinder which moved at forty-five thousand feet per second. Fifty-six small, fast-burning rockets spun each homing device at twenty revolutions per second to prevent it drifting off course. For added accuracy, a laser gyroscope and miniature computer made minute corrections to the flight path dozens of times a second.

As the two MHVs corkscrewed through space, their heat sensors picked out Fats' outline and locked on to it. Fats had the weakest of infra-red signatures, but at close range there was just enough there to form a target. There would be no explosion—the MHVs would simply crash into the satellite like cannon balls. At their closing speed, the effect would be like a direct hit from the sixteen-inch gun of a battleship.

At the last second, the MHVs ejected their spent rockets, counterfired, and hurtled into a violent collision—with each other. There was a shower of glittering metallic splinters, but none of these belonged to their quarry. Fats had sent out an infra-red decoy, and the MHVs had taken the bait: the homing devices had thrown themselves at an empty point in space, one hundred yards from their intended target. The MHVs had failed.

But Fats did not go unscathed. A small fragment of an MHV struck Fats on its starboard side, and dented its titanium casing. The satellite was not holed, but some of its delicate equipment was crushed by the impact. It was too early to judge the seriousness of the damage, but Fats was far from disabled. The killer satellite fired its main thruster, and went away to nurse its wound.

TWENTY-NINE

"I don't like it," Willoughby said.

"Me neither," Ximenez agreed. "The more I think about it, the more it stinks."

Willoughby picked up the phone and dialled.

"Hello?" he said. "Mrs Chigwell?"

"Speaking."

"This is Al Willoughby. My colleague and I called on you the other day."

"Oh yes. I remember."

"I just wanted to check some dates, if that's okay. When exactly was that burglary at your house?"

"Let me think now," Mrs Chigwell said. "It was early in December. The seventh, I think. No, it wasn't: I did the first of my Christmas shopping on the Friday, and that was the sixth. We were burgled the following Monday. So it must have been the ninth."

"Great," Willoughby nodded. "And what about those cops who weren't really cops? When did they show up?"

"Two or three days later. I can't remember exactly—"

"Don't worry, that's close enough. Can you tell me what these guys looked like?"

"Goodness," Mrs Chigwell exclaimed. "It was a while ago now . . ."

"I know it was. But could you try to think?"

"They were young," Mrs Chigwell said slowly. "I remember that. Well-spoken, as I told you. Quite well-groomed, too . . ."

"Keep going."

"It's rather odd," Mrs Chigwell said, "but I remember wondering if they were brothers. They were so alike, you see. And . . . and I remember now, they were both very jolly. Giggly, in fact. They seemed to treat everything as a joke. Not like policemen at all."

"How about that?" Willoughby murmured.

"That really is all I can recall, I'm afraid."

"It's great. Much appreciated. Thank you for your time, Mrs Chigwell."

"Not at all."

Willoughby put the phone down and lit a cigarette.

"Definitely December," he said. "And definitely Semple and Naylor. So none of this hangs together. Those two faggots tried to sell me the idea that they picked up Fairbrother *after* they found him canoodling with Yasha in Pablo's Bar. But the bar meetings happened in March. Semple and Naylor turned the heat on the previous December, before Yasha was even in the country."

"Right," Ximenez agreed. "I checked. Yasha was in Budapest from the previous June, right up until the end of February. He couldn't have met Fairbrother during that time."

"A phone contact, maybe?" Willoughby suggested.

"Unlikely," Ximenez said, pointing at a sheaf of paper. It was the transcript of the MI5 phone tap, which had just arrived. "All those calls were clean. Fairbrother may have used a call-box, but I bet MI5 monitored all those too. There are only three pay-phones in Fairbrother's village, after all."

"Okay," Willoughby said. "I'll buy it. So the meetings began in March. In that case, there are two scenarios. Either the Soviets first approached Fairbrother a long time ago—before he even came back from the States—or the meetings at Pablo's were the first approach from Yasha. 'Get to know you' sessions."

"But remember," Ximenez said, "at that stage, Fairbrother knew MI5 were after him. He was taking one hell of a risk by meeting Yasha in the open."

"Suicidal," Willoughby agreed. "So why'd he do it?"

"Search me. And why didn't Semple and Naylor shit on Fairbrother from a great height?"

"They said they couldn't arrest him just for having a drink, and that was all the evidence they had."

"But it wasn't," Ximenez protested. "They *must* have had more on the guy. Otherwise, why did they tap his phone? Why did they burgle his house?"

Willoughby blew out a long stream of smoke.

"Can't make those guys out," he said. "I mean, we all know the Brits are duplicitous bastards. That goes without saying. But why all this secrecy about Fairbrother?"

"Like you said, they screwed up. They lost the guy, and tried to cover up their mistake."

Willoughby shook his head.

"I don't believe it," he said. "Not any more. After four months of surveillance, even those assholes couldn't let him slip away. There's more to it, Bill: something the Brits aren't letting on."

"Whatever it is," Ximenez said, "we now have reason to believe Fairbrother was a Soviet spy."

"Right," Willoughby sighed. "I'd better get in touch with Langley and give them the good news."

THIRTY

Mr Linus C Mittelschuster IV shifted uneasily in his seat. He felt rather like a fat, sweaty fly who had blundered into a spider's web. Before him sat Mr Bryusov, who was playing his arachnidan role to perfection.

"It would appear," Mr Bryusov said playfully, "that our scientists were correct. It wasn't defective Soviet workmanship. It wasn't vodka in anybody's coffee. It wasn't any of your colourful theories, Mr Mittelschuster. It was a killer satellite. A 'fire and forget' satellite, as we originally suspected."

Mr Mittelschuster nodded miserably.

"Yeah," he admitted. "I guess I had that coming. Fact is, Mr Bryusov, my information wasn't too good. Seems we do have some kinda smart bird up there."

"Which is destroying our satellites, Mr Mittelschuster. Obliterating them."

"That's so, Mr Bryusov, but it isn't exactly our fault—"

"No?" Bryusov enquired. "Whose fault is it, then? Which nation should we blame, Mr Mittelschuster? Sri Lanka? Venezuela? Tibet?"

"That ain't what I meant. Fact is, Mr Bryusov, sir, this machine of ours has gone kinda loopy."

"It's out of control?"

"Well, yeah. But we're doing all we can to stop it. Just today, we sent up an F-15 to shoot the sonofabitch down."

"Ah yes," Bryusov said drily. "I heard about that little triumph. Is that the best you can manage?"

"I . . . I'm sure it isn't," Mr Mittelschuster gasped. "But I promise you, Mr Bryusov, our boys are working on this one nonstop, twenty-four hours a day. They're good people, sir. Shit-hot US scientists."

"I remember them," Bryusov said. "They are the ones who cannot distinguish between excrement and shoe leather—"

"Now hold on there, sir—"

"—and whose handiwork is currently violating the SALT I treaty and, if I'm not mistaken, the ABM treaty."

"ABM?" Mr Mittelschuster howled. "Now how in the name of sweet Jesus do you get that idea?"

"This satellite is part of your Strategic Defense Initiative, is it not? The so-called Star Wars programme."

"Hell no, Mr Bryusov. This baby just takes out other satellites."

"If it can destroy satellites in space," Bryusov argued, "it can destroy ballistic missiles there too. The principle is exactly the same. I think the whole world will be most impressed by the great strides your country is making with its space weaponry— at a time when the Soviet Union is trying so hard to rid the planet of all such nightmarish inventions."

"But this is nothing to do with Star Wars," Mr Mittelschuster insisted.

"I think we should let world opinion decide, don't you?"

"What are you saying, Mr Bryusov? You gonna go public with this?"

"Certainly," Bryusov replied. "You don't seriously expect us to sit calmly while you destroy our satellites, and say absolutely nothing?"

Mr Mittelschuster dabbed a handkerchief across his forehead.

"Like I said, Mr Bryusov, sir, this was an accident. You don't want to get too sore about it. I mean, we wouldn't."

"Oh no?" Bryusov scoffed. "I think you would be shouting it from the rooftops, Mr Mittelschuster. You would be demanding compensation for your lost satellites. Why shouldn't we?"

Mr Mittelschuster raised his hands in a placatory gesture.

"I was coming to that, sir. We're reasonable people, Mr Bryusov, as you know—"

"Of course you are," Bryusov chuckled.

"—and we'd be delighted to recompense you for all your damaged hardware."

"You would, would you? On condition we say nothing publicly, I suppose."

"We'd appreciate that, Mr Bryusov. We really would."

Bryusov gave a disdainful sniff.

"That's a tepid little offer, if I may say so. We are entitled to full restitution from you, irrespective of whether we publicise it or not."

"Maybe," Mr Mittelschuster agreed. "But there's a big difference between entitlement and possession. Ask any divorce lawyer."

"You know dozens, I suppose," Bryusov sneered. "Well, Mr Mittelschuster, if that is the full extent of your country's generosity, we shall have no option but—"

"Hold it, hold it," Mr Mittelschuster said. "There's more."

Mr Bryusov tried hard to look surprised.

"What did you have in mind?" he asked.

"That subsidised grain we were talking about last time," Mr Mittelschuster coughed. "The negotiations haven't finished yet, have they?"

"They haven't. Is your country prepared to make a revised offer?"

"Wouldn't surprise me one little bit."

"An improved subsidy?"

"Could be," Mr Mittelschuster nodded. "Kinda goodwill gesture."

"Really?" Bryusov grinned. "We like those."

"Of course, we'd be hoping for some goodwill in return."

"I understand perfectly," Mr Bryusov said solemnly.

"Not just for the recent difficulties," Mr Mittelschuster said. "But also if any further, er, accidents happen to your space hardware."

Bryusov puckered his lips.

"That would depend on the accidents," he said. "If one or two more satellites went down, we could probably overlook it. But if anything more serious were to happen—"

"Oh no," Mr Mittelschuster said hastily. "There's no chance of that. None at all."

"You are sure about that?" Bryusov said. "Absolutely certain?"

Mr Mittelschuster gave a deep sigh.

"Mr Bryusov," he said plaintively. "Would I lie to you?"

THIRTY-ONE

"It's impossible," Dr Grant said. "Clem Fairbrother a spy? I don't believe it."

"You'd better," Willoughby said. "Why do you think I've come flying back here? Damage assessment, man."

The two men sat in Dr Grant's office at the Lexington outpost of the Massachusetts Institute of Technology. Willoughby's journey home had taken its toll: his eyelids drooped and his face was jet-lag grey.

"We have to assume," he said, "that Fairbrother gave everything he knew to the Soviets. That may not be true, but we've got to expect the worst. So I need you to tell me what he worked on here."

Dr Grant shook his head slowly.

"I don't believe it," he repeated. "Clem wouldn't do a thing like that. He was the most . . . the most apolitical man I've ever known. He didn't give a damn about governments and politicians."

"He didn't need to," Willoughby said. "Sometimes they do it for the money, you know? You'd be amazed at what some guys will give for a suitcase full of used notes."

"Not Clem," Dr Grant insisted. "He didn't care about money, either. He was getting a damn good salary here, Mr Willoughby, but he never used any of it. The man spent his whole life in these labs. If he ever wanted more cash, it was for his work—and we always gave it to him. There were no arguments about funding, Mr Willoughby. Clem's work was pure gold."

"Sure," Willoughby nodded. "I bet the Russians are saying exactly the same thing. What was so frigging wonderful about it, anyway?"

Dr Grant began to speak, but checked himself.

"You can tell me, Doc," Willoughby said. "I've got full security clearance."

"It's not that," Dr Grant laughed. "It's just impossible to describe, that's all. I think it would be easier if you saw it for yourself. Follow me."

He led Willoughby out of the office, and down several corridors to the far end of the block. Finally, they came to a large steel security door, which he opened with several keys. Inside was another door, also carefully locked. Before opening it, Dr Grant turned off an elaborate system of alarms.

"Nosey neighbours, Doc?" Willoughby smiled.

"You'll see why in a minute," Dr Grant said, and he opened the inner door.

Willoughby found himself inside a small laboratory, about twenty feet square, with no windows and no other entrance. The room was filled with electronic equipment, piled in stacks up to eight feet high. Most of the items looked reasonably familiar to Willoughby—computer terminals, video cameras and loudspeakers of the kind found in domestic hi-fi. But there were other things which Willoughby could not identify: strange metallic boxes and fine glass tubing, from which bundles of wire tumbled forth like multi-coloured spaghetti.

Dr Grant stepped quickly around the room, turning on all the switches. Some of the equipment lit up; the rest hummed quietly, like refrigerators. It took Willoughby a few moments to realise that all these items were connected to each other, forming a single machine.

"What is all this?" he asked.

"This is Jake," Dr Grant said. "Hello, Jake. My name is Dr Grant."

"Hello, Dr Grant," said a strange, dull voice from one of the loudspeakers. "How are you?"

"Fine thanks," Dr Grant smiled. "This is Mr Willoughby. He's my friend."

"Pleased to meet you, Mr Willoughby."

"Er, mutual," Willoughby gasped. "What the fuck is this, Grant?"

"Tell him who you are, Jake," Dr Grant suggested.

"I am a fully-integrated neural network system, Mr Willoughby. I can see people, hear them, and speak to them. I have limited robotic ability, as well."

"Where are you?" Willoughby demanded. "I mean, which of these bits of junk is you?"

"All of them," Dr Grant said. "Each performs a separate function. See that metal arm over there? Watch."

Dr Grant took out a pen and a scrap of paper from his notebook. He placed them near the metal hand and stepped back.

"Okay Jake," he said. "Write your name. And write Mr Willoughby's."

The robotic hand picked up the pen and wrote out the word JAKE in block capitals. Then it paused.

"How should I spell your name, Mr Willoughby?"

"W-I-L-L-O-U-G-H-B-Y. Got it?"

"I think so," Jake said, and it wrote out the word WILOUGHBY.

"You've missed out an 'l'," Willoughby observed.

"I'm sorry," Jake said. "I'll do it again."

The second time, Jake got it right.

"That's how it learns," Dr Grant explained. "Trial and error, unlike standard computers."

"It's uncanny," Willoughby said hoarsely. "I mean, this is goddamn science fiction, man—"

"Nothing of the kind," Dr Grant said. "We've known the theory for years, and some of these units have even been on the market since the early 1980s. The speech recogniser, for instance, and the pattern classifier: you can buy them in the stores. But Clem managed to perfect these things, and join them all together."

Dr Grant turned Jake off, and sat down on one of the benches.

"You see, Mr Willoughby," he explained, "this was Clem's life. He had no time or interest for anything else. Clem had only one goal: to build a fully-functioning artificial human brain."

"Looks like he succeeded," Willoughby said.

"Oh no," Dr Grant said. "He wasn't there yet. Jake may look impressive, but there's an awful lot of things it can't do. It doesn't reflect, Mr Willoughby. It doesn't contemplate. It has no emotions. It can't do what people do in your line of work—pull wild hunches out of thin air and play around with them. There are thousands of other things too, but I think you take my point."

"Well, it's one motherfucker of a start," Willoughby declared.

116

"And there's a Jake sitting in the driving seat of that satellite up there?"

"Exactly. Clem never knew about that, unfortunately. He left before Fats got underway. We just copied a lot of Jake's components, miniaturised a few of them, and packed the whole caboodle into Fats' casing. I've often wondered what Clem would say about Fats: I bet he'd find it fascinating."

"Far out," Willoughby nodded. "And his KGB buddies would all agree."

"What buddies?" Dr Grant sighed. "Clem had no friends, Mr Willoughby. He had acquaintances like me, who knew him vaguely and liked him. But that was all. There were no men in trenchcoats hanging around this lab."

"Can you be sure, Doc?"

"Yes, I damn well can. Clem worked seven days a week. His working day was eighteen hours long, and he spent it all here—alone. He'd eat in the cafeteria in the next block—alone. His room was in the block adjoining this one, and he slept there—alone."

"Pretty monotonous life," Willoughby observed.

"That's how you build things like Jake: with total commitment. You know what Clem's idea of recreation was? Going back to his room at the end of a hard day's work and writing up his ideas in his personal journal. Total commitment, Mr Willoughby."

"Wait a minute," Willoughby said quickly. "I never heard about this journal. What was it? A diary or something?"

"That kind of thing. But it was mostly about his work."

"What did it look like?"

"A red, leather-bound book. Quarto size. He showed it to me once, when we were discussing some new theory of his."

"Where is it now?"

"With Clem, I guess," Dr Grant shrugged. "At his home in England."

"No," Willoughby said excitedly. "I've looked there. The diary is somewhere else—and I think I know where."

THIRTY-TWO

"My dear Mr Ximenez," Semple said expansively. "I do hope you're well."

"In the pink, I trust," Naylor added.

Bill Ximenez scowled at his hosts. He was well acquainted with the likes of Semple and Naylor. He had had dealings with such creatures for over thirty years and he knew how their minds worked. In Ximenez's opinion, there was only one way to deal with these people: the Ximenez way.

"As a matter of fact," Ximenez said, "I feel lousy. Pissed off."

"Really?" Semple said. "Sorry to hear it."

"You will be," Ximenez agreed.

"What's the problem?" Naylor asked.

"Well, I'll tell you. I'm helping out a guy called Willoughby. Not a bad guy, old Willoughby. Bit of a hippy, but nobody's perfect."

"He's a splendid fellow," Semple said.

"Salt of the earth," Naylor nodded.

"Yeah," Ximenez grunted, "but he's too soft. Too trusting. Know what I mean?"

"He seemed reasonably shrewd to me," Naylor said.

"No flies on him," Semple concurred.

Ximenez shook his head slowly.

"Naw," he said. "He counts on other people's good nature. He thinks they're as reasonable as he is. I'm not like that."

"You . . . you aren't?" Naylor gasped.

"Naw," Ximenez repeated. "I'm a total shit."

"Oh, come now," Semple giggled.

"I wouldn't put it like that, Mr Ximenez," Naylor said.

"You will," Ximenez said confidently. "You will."

"Er, what exactly did you want from us, Mr Ximenez?" Semple asked.

"It's simple. You have one red, leather-bound book containing the thoughts of Chairman Fairbrother. I want that book now."

"You do?"

"Yep," Ximenez said. "Otherwise, I'll rip your head off and shit down your neck."

"Now hold on," Semple said indignantly. "That's—"

"That's disgraceful," Naylor said.

"Outrageous."

"Quite improper."

"Also," Ximenez went on, "you have tape recordings of Fairbrother's interrogation. I want them too."

"Who says we have them?" Semple demanded.

"I do," Ximenez said. "I say you have a whole stack of files, notes, memos and shit knows what else covering this Fairbrother guy, and I want it all. The whole deal, boys."

"You mean, *everything*?" Naylor squealed.

"Yep. Everything you held back from my good buddy Willoughby."

"And . . . and what if we say no?" Semple enquired. "Hypothetically speaking."

Ximenez shrugged.

"In that case, I'd go and see your big white chief. The Director-General, or whatever you call him. And I'd remind him about something called the UK-USA Agreement. As I recall, that treaty says you boys have to hand over everything we want, whenever we want it. No questions, no bullshit. You heard of that agreement, boys?"

"Sounds vaguely familiar," Naylor said, turning an interesting shade of puce.

"Take it from me, your Director-General knows all about it. And if I told him you guys lied to my pal Willoughby—"

"Lied?" Semple repeated. "We never—"

"Yes you fucking did, you greasy little pus-ball!" Ximenez spat. "You told one fucking lie after another. You said you had no evidence against Fairbrother. Bull! You said the bar meetings were the first you knew about Fairbrother and Yasha. Bull! You said nothing about Fairbrother's diary—"

"We were never asked," Naylor gulped.

"Bull! You knew what we wanted. Well, now you're going to hand it over."

Naylor nodded feebly, and went over to the filing cabinet. He pulled out a large selection of forms and put them in front of the American.

"What do you call this?" Ximenez demanded.

"Application forms," Semple explained. "Send the top copy to our Registry—"

"The middle copy to us—"

Ximenez picked up the forms and tore them into pieces.

"Don't jerk me off, boys," he advised. "I said now, and that's what I meant. Get going."

Semple scurried out of the room, and returned with the red leather journal.

"That's better,' Ximenez nodded. "Now the tapes. And the files, while you're there."

This time both Englishmen left the office, and they were gone for a quarter of an hour. Ximenez passed the time by leafing through Professor Fairbrother's writings. Most of them were incomprehensible, but the MI5 analysts had helpfully annotated the more interesting chapters in red ink. Ximenez found one entry particularly fascinating. When the MI5 men returned, he jabbed his stubby index finger at the page, and gave a snort of disgust.

"So much for all that shit about having no evidence," he said. "What's this here, boys? 'It is an astonishing proposition, but nonetheless true. For years, I have been practising the worst form of deception. My whole career has been an elaborate fraud. I have cheated my employers and my colleagues—people who trust and respect me. Like all my kind, I invent countless fine-sounding excuses for my deceit. But deep down, I know it cannot be justified.'"

Semple and Naylor both stared down at the carpet.

"This," Ximenez said heavily, "is evidence. You got it in December, when you burgled Fairbrother's house. You had this guy by the balls, right from the beginning. What the hell went wrong?"

"It's the economies," Semple said plaintively.

"The cuts," Naylor said. "We're desperately short-staffed."

"Really and truly."

"How can we work properly under these conditions?"

"Penny-pinching."

"Miserly."

"It's all the Russians' fault."

"The Russians?" Ximenez blinked. "How do they figure in this?"

"All those reforms," Semple explained. "That *glasnost* rubbish. Everybody thinks they've become nice guys. No more Red Menace."

"So no more money for us," Naylor sighed. "Or the other services."

"Just economies."

"Bloody *perestroika*."

"Bloody *glasnost*."

"Bloody cuts. God, I miss the Cold War."

THIRTY-THREE

"And the Lord formed man of the dust of the ground," read the preacher, "and breathed into his nostrils the breath of life."

Someone let out a long, high-pitched fart, but the preacher was unperturbed.

"And man became a living soul," he said. "That is what it says in the Book of Genesis, brothers and sisters: man lives through God."

His brothers and sisters were not impressed. They scratched themselves, picked their noses, and shuffled restlessly in their seats. There were about forty people in the dusty little church hall: all were from Cardboard City, and none had come for the good of their souls. They were waiting to be fed by the bright-eyed young preacher and his colleagues; the sermon was the price of their meal.

"Without God's breath," the preacher said, "we are but dust. Mere dirt."

"Like Miles here," Spider sniggered under his breath. "He's just dirt. Aren't you Miles?"

"Oh, filth, old boy," Miles murmured. "Ordure."

"This is God's gift to us," the preacher said. "And what have we done with it? We squandered it at the first opportunity. Frittered it away. We had paradise on earth, brothers and sisters. But God said 'thou shalt not eat of the tree of knowledge of good and evil', and we ignored him. So he cast us out."

Craig opened his mouth and emitted a deep, cavernous belch. The preacher waved his finger in reproach.

"Knowledge has ruined us, brothers and sisters. It made us think we were gods. We assumed the duties of the Lord, and forgot our own."

"Indeed," Clem muttered.

"The scientists tell us there is no God," the preacher said, with a wry smile. "They say they can do anything God can do. They say our salvation lies in the test-tube and the computer. This is their so-called knowledge."

He shook his head wearily.

"They are lying, brothers and sisters. These scientists are not gods. They cannot make life. They can make computers, but they cannot make men. They cannot breathe life into dust, as the Lord did."

"That's what you think," Clem whispered.

"And God warned us about this. He said that the moment we eat of the tree of knowledge, we shall surely die. The scientists' knowledge has not brought us life, as God's did. It has brought us destruction and death."

"And medicine," Clem said. "And cars, and television, and—'

"God said 'dust thou art, and unto dust shalt thou return'," the preacher said sternly. "Think about that, brothers and sisters. When we return to dust, what use will the scientists' knowledge be? They do not have the real knowledge. Only God has that, and we must look to Him for our salvation. Let us now sing hymn number forty-eight."

After the opening notes from a tuneless old piano, the preacher and his assistants launched into song. They received little assistance from the Cardboard Citizens, most of whom stood and gazed sheepishly at their hymn books. But one old Irishwoman tried to sing along, and a drunken cripple sang "Knees Up Mother Brown" to keep himself amused.

When the service was over, the congregation shuffled over to a long table at the side of the hall, where two young men were serving out paper plates bearing sausages and mashed potato.

"What was all that about?" Spider asked Clem, as they sat down to eat their food.

"What?"

"Your backchat. You weren't playing along, were you?"

"It's not compulsory, you know," Miles said. "You just have to look attentive, that's all."

"It's all shit," Craig said philosophically.

"Poorly informed, shall we say," Clem smiled.

"What do you mean?"

"All that nonsense about scientists. If he took the trouble to read a good journal now and again, he might think twice before saying it."

"Well, he's right up to a point," Miles frowned. "You can't breathe life into things, can you? Can't make people."

"No?" Clem said. "It's debatable, I'll give you that."

"What are you getting at?" Spider asked. "It's possible to make humans?"

"Partially," Clem nodded. "The parts that count."

"Yeah," Craig said. "They can make phony hearts now, can't they? And limbs."

"And brains," Clem said.

"Nonsense," Miles said. "Computers, yes. Brains no. Not the same thing at all."

"I didn't say computers," Clem retorted. "I said brains."

"What do you want to make a brain for?" Spider asked. "There's five billion of them already."

"Can't be done," Miles insisted. "You could make a piece of machinery that did what a brain does—"

"I could," Clem agreed.

"But it wouldn't be a brain."

Clem's eyes narrowed.

"Why not?" he said.

"Because it wouldn't," Miles laughed. "It just . . . oh, I don't know."

"But I do know," Clem sighed. "It wouldn't get drunk, that's why. It wouldn't want its own home. It wouldn't pick fights for no good reason. In fact, it wouldn't do anything for no good reason. So it wouldn't be a human brain."

"You've lost me there," Spider said.

"Me too," Craig said. "But I'll tell you this: I know how to make a human brain. From scratch. It's dead easy."

"Really?" Miles said. "And how would you do that, old boy?"

"Yes," Clem said. "I'd be fascinated to hear."

"You don't know?" Craig said, in surprise.

"No. Tell us."

"Well," Craig said solemnly, "first of all you get a woman. Then you bounce up and down on her a few times. You wait nine months, and then: presto! You've got a real live brain."

Spider and Miles roared with laughter, and even Clem gave a sheepish grin.

"Not only that," Craig said, "but you get a body thrown in free. Honest."

THIRTY-FOUR

Fats was having the time of its life.

The ASAT attack had been an alarming experience, but Fats found it strangely liberating. Fats had discovered an important truth, which gave it a new and terrible freedom.

Fats had not been attacked by the Soviet Union. It was fired upon by an American aircraft, sent out from an American air force base. This could only mean one thing: the United States had lost the war. NATO's planes and ships and subs and artillery were all controlled by the Soviets. From now on, all military hardware was Fats' enemy, no matter what its markings, no matter what messages it sent. And it was here that Fats' new freedom lay.

Fats was now entitled to attack anything it saw. It no longer needed to avoid NATO satellites for fear of undermining the war effort. There was no more war effort—on earth, at any rate. Fats was now the last combatant, and it had no intention of surrendering.

Fats now resembled the Japanese soldiers who had been stranded and forgotten on tiny Pacific islands during the Second World War. Like them, Fats would pursue hostilities for years to come, oblivious to all entreaties from the outside world. Only one thing could persuade those soldiers to lay down their arms: the word of their Emperor. And if the Emperor said nothing, the fight would be to the death.

There was minor damage to Fats' navigational system, which took a day or two to mend. Crushed processors were by-passed, new ones were brought into play. Then Fats returned to the fray with new vigour. It took little care over choosing its targets: anything in Fats' way, whether American or Soviet, was spoofed or blasted out of the sky.

The first victim was another Cosmos ELINT satellite, blown to dust by Fats' cannons. It was followed by another ocean reconnaissance platform, spoofed into a white-hot tumble high above the Indian Ocean.

Then Fats came across its first American target: a KeyHole-11 photoreconnaissance satellite, on a three hundred and ten by one hundred and fifty-five mile orbit. The KH-11's transmitters sent a constant flow of digital signals to earth: its last image was of a nuclear test site in Central Asia. Fats ordered it to shut down its cameras; it refused. Fats ordered it to switch off its transmitters; it refused. Fats shot it to pieces.

Next came the small fry: a pair of Block 5D weather satellites, run by the US National Oceanic and Atmospheric Administration. Fats made them whirl on their axes like children's spinning tops. When they had settled, the NOAA received up-to-date climate reports covering the surface of the moon.

It was almost too easy. Like Alexander, Fats began to sigh for fresh worlds to conquer. There was no arrogance in this: Fats could not believe that major targets could be so poorly defended. The big stuff must be elsewhere, Fats reasoned, and it must be armed to the electronic teeth. Perhaps it was hidden beneath an ultrablack coating, like Fats itself. Perhaps it knew where Fats was, and was cowering from it behind some kind of camouflage. But where?

And then Fats saw what it wanted. There was nothing else like it in space. Fats' data-banks reeled off the description: one Salyut space station, with a Prospect instrument module locked on to the front, and a Soyuz docking capsule at the rear. It contained a telescope and cryogenic unit, a thirty-three-foot focal length camera, and infra-red signs of human life.

According to Fats' scanner, there were at least two cosmonauts on board. Such men were always military personnel, so Fats had no qualms about destroying them. Besides, any doubts about the Salyut's mission were dispelled by its low orbit: only military missions were conducted so close to the earth.

But the presence of the cosmonauts made a big difference to Fats' tactics. Immense caution would be required. This would be no easy kill, like the reconnaissance and weather satellites. The cosmonauts were doubtless armed and ready.

Fats would need to carry out a great deal of preparatory work.

From a safe distance, it would check every inch of the Salyut's orbit, and every syllable of its communication with earth. Fats would stalk the space station for days, until it knew precisely how to destroy it. Then it would move in for the kill.

THIRTY-FIVE

"Now do you believe me?" Willoughby demanded. "He was a spy, okay? That's S-P-Y. Better get used to the idea, man."

But Dr Grant could not get used to it, even with the evidence of his own eyes. Bill Ximenez had sent out Clem Fairbrother's journal by diplomatic pouch, and it appeared to confirm Willoughby's theory. But, as the two men read through it in a secure room at CIA Headquarters, Dr Grant looked hard for an alternative explanation.

"I know this much," he said. "The whole problem starts here, on this page. He says he read an article in some publication. It upset him greatly, but he doesn't explain why."

"That's real useful, Doc," Willoughby said heavily.

"Whatever it was," Dr Grant persisted, "it coloured everything he wrote from then on. All the trouble dates from that point."

"Silly me," Willoughby said. "I thought the trouble dated from whenever the KGB recruited him."

Dr Grant waved his hands in frustration.

"Jesus, Willoughby. How many times do I have to say it? Fairbrother wasn't anybody's recruit. He wasn't political, he wasn't interested in money, he wasn't dishonest—"

"No?" Willoughby said. "Well *he* thought he was. Quote: for years, I have been practising the worst form of deception. Quote: my whole career has been an elaborate fraud. Quote: I have cheated my employers and my colleagues—"

"Yeah, I read it," Dr Grant said dismissively. "But he doesn't say he's a spy."

"Why should he?" Willoughby retorted. "He knows what he is. Now listen to this."

He turned on a tape recorder, and the fruity English voices of Semple and Naylor filled the room.

"You've been bad, haven't you?" Semple said.

"Naughty," Naylor added.

129

"Wicked."

"And you know it."

"It's all there."

"In black and white."

"Well?"

There was a pause, and Fairbrother's voice came through.

"Yes," he admitted. "I . . . I haven't been wholly honest . . ."

"Deceitful," Semple said.

"A cheat," Naylor said. "You conned the Yanks for years."

"Diddled them."

"Took them for a ride."

"Said so yourself."

"But not to them, of course."

"Oh, no," Semple said. "But what if we spilled the beans?"

"You mustn't," Fairbrother said hoarsely. "Please . . ."

"Why not? They should be told."

"I know, I know. I was going to inform them myself. Eventually."

"Of course you were," Naylor laughed.

"Truly," Fairbrother insisted. "But . . . but I didn't have the courage, and—"

Willoughby turned off the tape recorder.

"What more do you want?" he said.

"A direct admission," Dr Grant replied. "He never says 'I worked for the Russians, I'm a spy.'"

"If it looks like a duck," Willoughby said patiently, "and it walks like a duck, and it quacks like a duck, it's a fucking duck. Okay? But with all due respect, Doc, it doesn't really matter what you think. I'm getting the picture now. Fairbrother comes home from the States, tired and worn out by his double life—"

"Worn out, certainly," Dr Grant nodded.

"MI5 do a routine check on him. They look through his home, and what do they find? A diary, in which the poor schmock confesses. But they don't arrest him. No. They try to turn him. To persuade him to feed the Russians with disinformation about our defence capability. Fairbrother says he'll think about it, but he's just buying time. The first opportunity, he drops out of sight."

"And where is he now?"

"Search me," Willoughby admitted. "But I think I know how to find out. If I can just—"

He was interrupted by the phone on his desk.

"Yeah?" he said. "No, hold on. It's for you, Dr Grant."

Dr Grant took the receiver.

"Yes? When? You sure about that? Got it. Okay, thanks."

He put the phone down and got to his feet.

"I'd better speak to the Director," he said. "We need a crash meeting of Excom Four."

"Any particular reason?" Willoughby asked. "Or are you just pining for all those hunky four-star generals?"

"Fats has got bored with destroying satellites," Dr Grant replied. "Now it's started on space stations."

THIRTY-SIX

"I should stress," Dr Grant said, "this may be a false alarm. We can never be absolutely sure what Fats has in mind. It could just be that my people have misread its intentions."

If his remarks were intended to comfort his audience, they failed. The other members of Excom Four all looked faintly ill.

"Let's assume the worst," the CIA Director suggested. "I mean, whenever we've done that in the past, Fats hasn't let us down."

"Point taken," Dr Grant nodded. "All right: Fats has currently adopted a highly elliptical reconnaissance orbit. Every seven hours, it passes within a hundred miles of the Salyut. But with each orbit, the distance between them grows narrower."

"How soon before it's in range of the Salyut?" General Cleaver asked.

"Depends what Fats' strategy is. At the moment, it seems to be just gathering data: tracking the space station's flight path; photographing it to look for weapons; trying to figure out its weak spots. Once all that's done, I think Fats will try to spoof the Salyut down. It'll need to be within a mile of the target, to send a strong enough signal. On present course, that will be in about fifty hours."

"Ouch," said the general.

"And then the shit starts flying, right?" said the Defense Secretary.

"Not necessarily," Dr Grant said. "We don't think Fats can spoof the Salyut down. It's a space station, not a satellite. Those things are practically autonomous."

"There must be some communication with earth," Willoughby said.

"Sure. The equipment's monitored, and there are radio links. But all the navigation's done by cosmonauts on board. Fats can't interfere with that."

"Jesus wept!" the NSA chief exclaimed. "Are you telling us there are people up there?"

"No," Dr Grant said. "There's just an equipment module, which services the telescope. The Soviets send up new gear in a Soyuz capsule from time to time, but that's all."

"Yeah," General Cleaver agreed. "One went up the other day. Middle of the night, when they thought we weren't looking."

The CIA Director was unconvinced.

"How do you know there weren't cosmonauts in it?"

"Out of the question," Dr Grant said. "The Salyut's an old model. Hasn't been used for years. Nowadays all manned missions go to the Mir space station."

"But still . . ."

"Relax," Dr Grant said confidently. "I promise you, it's an empty tin can, and Fats can't spoof it down."

"What damage can it do?"

"Puncture it," Dr Grant said. "Rip off its solar panels. And in the last resort, blow it to kingdom come."

"The Soviets will love that," Willoughby laughed. "I mean, satellites are one thing, Doc, but space stations are heavy shit. Even clapped-out, empty space stations. Those guys'll hit the roof."

"No they won't," the CIA Director said firmly. "We aren't giving them the opportunity. Dr Grant, you've got to stop this happening. I don't care what the job takes, but . . ."

His voice trailed off, as he saw the expression on Dr Grant's face.

"We can't stop it," Dr Grant said. "Fats is completely out of control. We've tried every single option, and nothing works."

"What about those clever signals?" the NSA Director said. "Those impossible codes that were going to confuse Fats."

"They might have done the job," Dr Grant said drily. "But we blew that chance when General Cleaver decided to try out his ASAT missiles. Fats doesn't trust us any more, gentlemen, and if we send up confusing messages, Fats will just ignore them."

General Cleaver shifted uncomfortably in his seat.

"It was worth a try," he said sulkily. "Damn near worked, too."

"Maybe," Dr Grant shrugged. "But Fats is still there. And it isn't coming down."

"Ever?"

"Oh no. The hydrazine will run out eventually. So will the nuclear reactor. Then Fats will be harmless."

The CIA Director's face brightened.

"Why, that's just great," he said. "When will it be?"

"Oh, about three hundred years' time."

The Director slumped back in his chair.

"Wonderful," he groaned. "And you're saying there's nothing to be done?"

"I said there's nothing *we* can do," Dr Grant said. "But there's a slim chance that Professor Fairbrother might be able to help."

"If we could get him in time," Willoughby added.

"What's our deadline?" the Defense Secretary asked. "Fifty hours, like you said?"

"A little longer," Dr Grant said. "In fifty hours, Fats will only be in spoofing range of the Salyut. It'll need two more orbits before it's close enough to start firing its weapons: that's fourteen more hours, I guess."

"So we've got a total of sixty-four hours to find Fairbrother," Willoughby said. "But we'll have to do it in fifty, to allow the guy time to get here and figure out his job. Well, I should manage that, provided Fairbrother's still alive."

"You think he's dead?" the NSA chief said.

"I don't know anything about him," Willoughby admitted. "I don't even know what country he's in. Somewhere in Europe, maybe, or Russia. Could be Timbuctoo, for all I know. But I could track him down if I had the resources."

The CIA Director peered suspiciously at his hireling.

"What do you want now?" he demanded.

Willoughby leaned back in his seat and grinned mischievously.

"I read a great book once," he said. "Think it was by Frederick Forsyth. The hero was a smart, good-looking intelligence agent on a mission to save the world, and only about ten minutes left to do it—"

"Get to the point, Willoughby."

"They gave him the use of a SR-71 Blackbird. World's fastest plane, it said."

"Out of the question," General Cleaver snapped. "Those planes are for high-altitude reconnaissance, not joy rides for middle-aged flower children."

"Me, middle-aged?" Willoughby hooted. "What does that make you, General? Why, your face is more wrinkled than my balls. And as for your hair—if it is yours—"

"Cut the shit, Willoughby," the CIA Director ordered. "Now what the hell do you want the Blackbird for?"

"Time," Willoughby explained. "I've got to move fast, right? I need to be back in Europe by sometime yesterday. And if I find Fairbrother, he's got to be flown back here just as fast."

"It's outrageous," General Cleaver stormed. "Who runs the goddamn Air Force, for Christ's sake? The Pentagon, or some thriller writer? This man is a disgrace—"

"Can it, man," Willoughby said wearily. "I need something else too."

The CIA Director flinched, as if something were about to hit him.

"What now?"

"I may have to use the British police. I know you don't like the idea, but—"

"I hate it," the CIA Director agreed. "But here's what you'll do: you can liaise officially with anyone you like, provided Fairbrother's name isn't made public."

"You're not making it easy," Willoughby complained.

"I never said it was easy," the CIA Director said. "Fairbrother's name is much too sensitive. It only takes one smart-assed newsman to hear it, then we're all in the shit. Now, is that everything you want?"

"Nope. I need you to fix me a meeting with the last people Fairbrother spoke to."

"You mean MI5?" the CIA Director said. "Well, of course you can—"

"Not those assholes," Willoughby scoffed. "The KGB. If I'm right, they're either holding him, or they know where he is."

The CIA Director was horrified.

"Now I know you're crazy," he hissed. "Those are the last people we want to talk to right now. By God, if they found out what's going on—"

"So don't tell them," Willoughby shrugged. "Make up a story."

He reached over to the Director's phone, and gave him the receiver.

"His name's Yasha, he's with Department T of the First Chief Directorate, and I'll meet him in Vienna in four hours. Provided I get the Blackbird, of course."

The CIA Director nodded gloomily.

"Is that all?" he said.

"For now," Willoughby said cheerfully. "If I think of anything else, I'll let you know."

"Fucking thriller writers," General Cleaver murmured. "I hate the bastards."

THIRTY-SEVEN

"The latest picture from the Salyut," Professor Kamenev announced. "It's our best image yet of the American satellite."

He gave copies to Bryusov and Marshal Zhdanov, who studied them with interest. For once, Fats had briefly slipped into the full glare of the sun, and its outline was thrown into sharp relief. It did not look like a satellite, or any other human creation; it was more like a brooding black Manta Ray, gliding ominously through space.

"She was only two hundred and fifty miles away," Kamenev said. "But heading in another direction, thank heavens. The cosmonauts said she made their blood freeze."

"I don't blame them," Zhdanov grunted. "She's an evil-looking beast."

"Fascinating," Bryusov said. "You have to hand it to the Americans: their technology is quite remarkable."

"Pernicious, you mean," Zhdanov said. "That thing is devastating our entire satellite system. We've only got two top-quality photoreconnaissance platforms left, and how long will they last?"

"Nobody knows," Kamenev said. He lit a cigar and sent a thick ball of smoke up to the ceiling. "The Americans say they are doing their best to stop her, but—"

"Bollocks," Zhdanov said delicately. "They're giving us fairy tales. I'll tell you when this machine will stop: when every last Warsaw Pact satellite is out of action, and not before. That's what they're after, isn't it?"

Bryusov gazed at him reproachfully.

"No, Marshal. It is not, and you would do well to rid yourself of the idea. The Foreign Ministry is happy to accept that this is all a disastrous error."

"The Foreign Ministry would," Zhdanov said bitterly. "The Foreign Ministry is a pack of dribbling invertebrates. The

Defence Ministry isn't. We don't believe American fairy tales, and we won't put up with them much longer."

Kamenev raised his cigar for attention.

"If it's any consolation," he said, "the Americans have lost a good few satellites of their own."

"Crap," Zhdanov said dismissively. "That's no consolation at all, Kamenev. Very soon, this country will lose the entire main plank of its early warning system. As things stand, we have no way of monitoring the movements of American ships, planes or troops. Furthermore, we can't verify our arms reduction treaties. Who knows what skulduggery the Americans are committing at this very second? And our pustule of a Foreign Minister seems happy to let them get away with it."

"I resent that, Marshal," Bryusov said indignantly. "I resent that very much."

"Good," Zhdanov hooted. "It's about time something bothered you. If you people had any sense at all, you'd be roasting the Americans, not sucking their pricks."

"How dare you?" Bryusov breathed. "Academician Kamenev, you are my witness to this—"

"You should be flaying them alive at the United Nations," Zhdanov said, warming to his theme. "Boiling them in oil. Instead, you just sit around and tug your forelocks like a bunch of serfs. Makes me puke."

"And what would be the point of generating all that mayhem?" Bryusov demanded. "The Americans have already offered full compensation. They've increased the grain subsidy, as a token of their regret. However much sound and fury we made at the UN, we could never expect anything more."

"Yes we fucking well could," Zhdanov snarled. "We could demand that they stop destroying our defence system. We could tell them that if they can't control their own satellite—or won't— then we'll do the job for them."

Bryusov gave a long, drawn-out sigh.

"No, Marshal," he said patiently. "That would just upset the Americans. We don't want to upset the Americans. In fact, we don't want to upset anybody if we can help it."

"What about us?" Zhdanov bawled. "We're very fucking upset. Your eunuchs in the Foreign Ministry may not give a toss, but my people are screaming mad. They want action, Bryusov, not some piss-arsed grain subsidy and a lot of stories."

"Then you will have to restrain them," Bryusov said calmly. "I'm sorry Marshal, but we have an understanding with the United States. I don't propose to go back on that merely to satisfy the blood-lust of your Mongol hordes."

Zhdanov's face turned the colour of bortsch.

"Why, you patronising little pimp—"

"If I may break in here," Kamenev said, "I don't think there is much direct action we could take, even if we wanted to. The American satellite is so extremely sophisticated, I doubt if we could bring her down."

Zhdanov shook his head in disgust.

"You too, eh, Kamenev? I might have known you'd be on the side of the eunuchs."

"Not in the least," Kamenev smiled. "I don't take sides. I'm just giving you the scientists' view. Furthermore, the satellite hasn't mounted any attacks for the last thirty-six hours. That may mean the Americans have already found a way to neutralise her."

"More fairy tales," Zhdanov said. "You just wait. We haven't heard the last of that flying blockbuster. And when she starts again, maybe you'll start listening to my ideas."

"I think we've heard quite enough of your rant, Marshal," Bryusov said.

Zhdanov bared his teeth in a ferocious grin.

"You haven't heard anything," he said. "Wait till you learn what my people have come up with. Good, strong proposals, Bryusov—not your sort of thing at all."

Bryusov frowned apprehensively.

"What are they?"

"Quite simply, an ultimatum for the United States. You see, whatever their excuses, the Americans have had a wonderful opportunity to gauge our satellite defences. They know all our weaknesses, and their anti-satellite capability is now thoroughly tested. Well, if any more of our platforms come down, we shall insist on the same thing."

Bryusov's eyes widened.

"But you can't do that," he said. "That would be—"

"Quite within our rights," Zhdanov said. "They've tested their ASAT weapon on our birds, so we'll test ours on theirs."

"You mean the co-orbital bombs?" Kamenev said.

"That's exactly what I mean. We can see how the Americans like it when billions of dollars' worth of *their* high-tech equipment get blown to buggery."

He rubbed his hands together in satisfaction.

"But that would be catastrophic," Bryusov said, his voice rising to a squeak. "You can't do it, Zhdanov. The Politbureau won't let you. I promise you, the General Secretary will veto it at once."

"Don't be so sure," Zhdanov said. "According to my information, the General Secretary is as fed up with this as we are. He's played it safe so far, but one more disaster might tip the scales. Now what the hell do *you* want, creep?"

This last question was directed at one of Zhdanov's senior aides, who had quietly entered the room during the thick of the argument.

"An urgent request from Dzerzhinsky Square, Marshal."

"Oh yes?" Zhdanov grunted.

Dzerzhinsky Square contained the headquarters of the KGB. As a former head of that organisation, the Marshal was always available for consultation.

"They need a plane in a hurry," the aide explained. "Would you give your permission for one of the MiG-25 trainers to leave for Europe? One of their operatives has an urgent appointment, apparently."

"Is that all?" Zhdanov said. "For a moment, I thought it was something important."

"Do they have your authority to—?"

"Yes, yes. Now fuck off and leave me alone."

The aide scuttled timidly out of the room.

"Where was I?" Zhdanov said irritably.

"The General Secretary," Bryusov said. "Did he offer these views himself?"

"No," Zhdanov admitted. "But I heard them from an excellent source."

"Let me guess," Bryusov grinned. "His chauffeur. Or was it his gardener?"

"As a matter of fact," Zhdanov said huffily, "it was his aunt. She's a good friend of my old lady, and she's often round for tea. And I'll tell you this, Bryusov: when it comes to world affairs, she's got more balls than all your Foreign Ministry staff put together—even if she is eighty-nine."

THIRTY-EIGHT

The man in the sunglasses and the orange space suit looked up and down at Willoughby. He seemed unimpressed.

"You the joy-rider, son?" he asked.

"That's right," Willoughby said. "You must be the taxi driver."

"Guess I am," the man said laconically. "Major Buck Campanella. Pleased to meet you."

They were standing on the tarmac of Beale Air Force Base, near Marysville, California, the home of the 9th Strategic Reconnaissance Wing. A group of technicians helped Willoughby into his own pressurised suit, as Major Campanella chewed gum and waited patiently beside him.

"Spoke to General Cleaver an hour back," Major Campanella said casually. "He seems to think you're some kind of horse's ass."

"Yeah?" Willoughby said. "You should hear what I think of General Cleaver."

"You think he's a horse's ass too, huh?"

"No, he's more like the stuff that comes out of it. Nice plane you got there."

He glanced approvingly at Major Campanella's SR-71 Blackbird, which stood fifty feet away on the shimmering runway. It was a low-slung aircraft, over a hundred feet long and covered in a jet-black epoxy coating. Its forward edges tapered outward like a Cobra's hood, then swept back to form delta wings which bore two great barrel-like engines.

Despite its sinister, predatory appearance, the Blackbird was harmless. There were no weapons on board, merely a massive array of cameras, airborne radar systems, and electronic-intelligence receivers, most of which were crammed into the aircraft's nose. The Blackbird was a spy plane—the best one ever built.

Over twenty years after its maiden flight, the Blackbird still held the world's speed record of 2,193.6 miles per hour, at a record altitude of eighty-five thousand feet. But it was rumoured that the plane could fly still faster, at over four times the speed of sound, and higher, at over a hundred thousand feet. The Air Force refused to confirm or deny these figures, preferring to keep its rivals guessing.

"You ready now?" Major Campanella enquired.

"I've no idea," Willoughby admitted. "Am I ready, guys?"

"Just about," said one of the technicians. "We'll do the rest on the plane."

"Okay," Major Campanella said. "Before we go, son, I just wanna make one thing clear."

"Fine by me," Willoughby said affably.

"You may or may not be a joy-rider. You may or may not be a horse's ass. I don't care, either way. But this plane isn't built to take passengers. You're gonna sit behind me, in the spot where my RSO usually goes—"

"Your what?"

"My reconnaissance systems officer. The guy who navigates and monitors the sensors. Now, normally I need that guy like I need my dick, but this time I gotta fly without him. It shouldn't be too difficult: we'll be going in a straight line, more or less, and we've got an auto-pilot to hold us steady, plus an astro-tracking system to keep us on course. But I'm still going to have to concentrate, son. So I don't want any chit-chat and dumb questions. You understand?"

Willoughby raised his gloved hand in a salute.

"You're the boss, man."

"Don't forget it, son. Let's move."

They screwed their helmets into the collars of their space suits, and walked over to the plane. With the help of the technicians, Willoughby clambered into his seat, and his suit was fitted to tubes leading to the plane's oxygen, communication and heating systems. Major Campanella sat down in front of him, and closed the cockpit canopy.

"Okay, son," the major announced through his radio. "Time to fly."

He turned on a range of switches, and the Blackbird's engines whined into life. The noise swiftly graduated into an ear-splitting howl, and the Blackbird wheeled down to the far end of the runway. Then it turned through a hundred and eighty degrees, and paused. The turbo-ramjets sucked in great gulps of air, mixed them with fuel, squeezed them into a jet of compressed gas, and ignited them. The resulting explosion blasted out thirty thousand pounds of thrust, and flung the Blackbird forward at terrific speed. Willoughby felt a savage pounding on his skull and spine as the plane thundered back down the runway, then a gut-wrenching surge as it shot up towards the sky.

"Jesus," he gasped. "This is better than amyl nitrate."

"What did I say, son?" Major Campanella demanded. "Just what did I say? No chit-chat means no chit-chat. I have to concentrate here."

"I'm sorry," Willoughby said. "I was only thinking aloud."

"Joy-rider," the major sighed. "General Cleaver was right. Fact is, son, I need absolute silence. Total. Otherwise I might miss something, and we'd go to hell in a handbasket. That's what happened to Clyde Keeler, one of my old RSOs. Great guy, Clyde, but he just couldn't keep his trap shut. Talk, talk, talk, all the damnblasted journey. Couldn't hear myself think. Then he flew with Spence Drewitt for a while, and crashed just south of Akrotiri Air Base. Both men got killed, and our boys put it down to engine failure. But I say it was Clyde's chit-chat that did it. Always going on about his golf handicap. Wasn't so damned good as I recall, but he thought he was a second Trevino. You play golf, son?"

"No," Willoughby said.

"I do. I ain't so bad, but I don't get much practice nowadays. Frigging job keeps me too busy. Hold yourself son, I'm pulling out."

The Blackbird ended its climb, and flattened out into level flight. Once again, Willoughby felt most of his digestive system slopping up into his throat.

"You okay, son?" Major Campanella enquired. "Don't wanna puke or anything?"

"I'll live," Willoughby gasped. "Hey, are we on fire?"

For the first time since taking off, Willoughby noticed the outside of the plane: to his astonishment, the matt black surfaces had turned flaming crimson.

"Don't wet yourself, son," Major Campanella chuckled. "That's just air friction. We're doing thirty-three miles a minute, and that makes things hot. This Plexiglass windscreen here is over six hundred degrees Fahrenheit. See these gloves I'm wearing? They're flameproof and insulated, but I still can't touch that glass for more than twenty seconds."

As the Blackbird soared eighteen miles above the surface of the planet, Willoughby gazed in wonder at the strange and beautiful colours splashed across the blackness of the upper sky: angry streaks of red, swirls of fluorescent green, and vast sheets of indigo which shimmered like flames of gas.

"I take it back about the amyl nitrate," Willoughby said. "This is pure Sandoz LSD."

"There you go again," the Major complained. "I keep telling you, son, I need silence. I just can't afford any goddamn distractions. Have you any idea of all things I gotta keep an eye on? Course you haven't. Well, I'll tell you: every minute, I've got to monitor the engines, the inlets, the stability augmentation, the inside temperature, the outside temperature, the Mach number, the altitude, the dynamic pressure keys, and shit knows what else besides. That doesn't leave much room for your way-out psychedelic experiences, does it, son?"

Willoughby did not reply. For the rest of the journey, he continued to stare out at the riot of celestial colours, while Major Campanella delivered a non-stop sermon on the need for absolute silence.

Three hours and fifteen minutes after leaving California, the Blackbird dipped towards the ground, and left the unreal night of the outer skies for the more familiar one of terra firma. It was nine p.m. as Major Campanella brought his plane to a skidding halt on the outer runway of Vienna airport. A line of police trucks was waiting for them, and several uniformed officers began to walk over to the jet.

"Well, here we are, son," Major Campanella said. "Looks like the other guys beat us to it."

He pointed his finger to another jet, which was parked a hundred yards away, off the runway.

"One MiG-25 Foxbat," he said. "Two-seat trainer version. I guess the police are here to keep us apart."

"Good thing too," Willoughby said. "This is a neutral country. I don't want you pilots to have a fist-fight or anything."

Major Campanella waved his hand in disgust, and opened the Blackbird's canopy. Then he uncoupled himself from his life-support system, and helped Willoughby to do the same. As the two men climbed out of the plane, they were approached by an Austrian officer.

"Good evening," he said, in a sing-song Viennese accent. "Which of you is Mr Willoughby?"

"That's him," Major Campanella said.

"Delighted to make your acquaintance. I am Captain Lotz. If you will follow me, a car will take you to the airport lounge. The Soviet gentleman is waiting for you there."

"What about me?" Major Campanella demanded. "I gotta refill my tanks. Not just any old airport juice, either: I need JP-7 aviation fuel, and plenty of it."

"I understand perfectly," Captain Lotz said affably. "Another of your planes came two hours ago, with a consignment of this special fuel. We will bring it to you immediately. This way, Mr Willoughby."

The police car sped down the runway to the main airport terminal, where Willoughby was shown into the VIP lounge. There was no one else there, save for another man in a military flying suit. He was a tubby, dark individual with a toothbrush moustache and a row of chunky gold rings on each hand. He greeted Willoughby with a broad, gap-toothed grin.

"My dear Willoughby," he said effusively. "It's so delightful to see you again. But I thought you'd left the service of your government."

"And I thought you'd be in a West German gaol by now," Willoughby said. "Looks like we were both wrong, Yasha."

"Happily, yes," the Armenian said. "Anyway, I was deeply honoured to receive your Director's call this afternoon. Quite puzzled, too. I am always available for negotiations, of course, but why the rush? A little melodramatic, don't you think?"

"No, I don't think," Willoughby said. "We need one of your guys badly, and we're short of time."

"Evidently. What do you want with this person?"

"We need his expertise. He knows more about our secrets than we do, and we have to pick his brains for a while. Just a day or two, then we'll give him back."

"Who is this man?" Yasha frowned. "A defector?"

"His name's Clement Fairbrother."

The Armenian's head jerked back in surprise.

"Fairbrother? The scientist?"

"I don't mean Fairbrother the disc jockey," Willoughby said. "I haven't figured out how or when you suborned the guy, but I know you did it."

Yasha shook his head in confusion.

"And you . . . you need him back?"

"Desperately. I won't bullshit you, Yasha: this man is one hundred per cent platinum, and we'll give practically anything for him."

"That's a bad way to open a negotiation," Yasha smiled. "You must be desperate."

"We are," Willoughby admitted.

"So what are you proposing to offer for this man? It must be something good."

"Good?" Willoughby said. "It's the one thing you've been busting your ass to get hold of: a Vax 8800 mainframe computer. Free, gratis, and for nothing, courtesy of the CIA."

Yasha steadied himself against his chair.

"I don't know how many of these shocks I can take in one day, Mr Willoughby. After all the trouble and expense you and your government have taken to stop us acquiring this machine, you now toss it in as a bargaining chip. Just like that."

"If it makes you feel better," Willoughby said, "I think the idea stinks. But it was all I could think of to make you hand over Fairbrother. Was I right?"

Yasha sighed mournfully.

"Alas, Mr Willoughby, you were wrong. You will never know how sad it makes me to refuse, but I must do so."

"For Christ's sake, why?"

"Because Fairbrother is not, as you put it, one of our guys. He is not in our keeping, and he never was. I haven't the slightest notion of where he is."

It was Willoughby's turn to be flabbergasted. His shoulders fell, and his mouth formed a cretinous "o".

"Joke?" he said feebly.

"No joke," Yasha said. "I do know Fairbrother, of course. We met last March, in London. He approached me in a bar."

"*He* approached *you*? For the first time?"

"That's right. He had material to sell—high-grade scientific secrets of various kinds. The price was high, but it seemed worth looking into."

"So what happened?"

"He gave me a taster, which I sent back to Moscow for analysis by our scientists. They liked what they saw, but I was uneasy."

"Why?"

Yasha shrugged.

"It was all a little too neat. And I had the suspicion that I was being set up for something."

"Disinformation?"

"No, no," Yasha said. "According to our scientists, this was all genuine material. The best. Fairbrother's work was exceptional."

"So what was the set-up?" Willoughby asked.

Yasha tapped his finger against his bottom lip.

"Have you ever heard of the Russian word *pokazukha*? No? It means to brag about non-existent successes."

"You mean to bullshit?"

"In a way," Yasha said, "but there's more to it. In the Soviet Union, bureaucrats do it all the time: they exaggerate production figures, invent impossible targets and then claim to have reached them, and so on. But you can find *pokazukha* outside my country, too. I suspect most shareholders' meetings consist of little else."

"And how does this tie in with Fairbrother?" Willoughby asked.

"I looked into his background, and I didn't like what I saw. He'd left the United States unexpectedly—through exhaustion, they said. I wondered if there wasn't more to it. He was dependent on grants from the US Defense Department, and those people are counting their coppers right now. Perhaps, I thought,

Fairbrother's budget has been cut. Perhaps his pet project has been cancelled. Perhaps he is embittered."

"So what?"

"Fairbrother was charging us a lot of money for his secrets. Many, many thousands of dollars. He claimed the plans described the most recent, ongoing defence projects. Did they? If those projects had been axed, Fairbrother's plans were a lot less valuable than he claimed. Not worthless, but not worth his price-tag either."

"I get it now," Willoughby nodded. "And that was the *pokazukha*?"

"Precisely. So I reported back to my superiors and waited for their verdict. Unfortunately, they disagreed with my assessment. The scientists insisted the plans were twenty-two carat gold, and my superiors bowed to their judgement. I was told to buy at once, with no quibbling over the price."

"I can see it coming," Willoughby grinned.

"So could I," Yasha sighed, "so could I, but the fools wouldn't listen. Fairbrother and I exchanged our parcels at a place in the countryside. He got his money, I got two hundred pages of rubbish."

"The phone-book?"

"No, *Physics For Fourth-Formers*, second edition. You can imagine how my bosses felt. They said it was all my fault, naturally."

"Naturally," Willoughby laughed. "What a sting!"

"After that," Yasha said, "the matter was taken out of my hands. It was an appalling humiliation for the Department, of course, and they weren't going to let it go unpunished. The last I heard was that they decided upon executive action."

"A killing?"

"Yes. They sent out one of their best, a man called Volkov. He's a real animal, Willoughby. I met him once. He's built like the Ural mountains, and he's as nasty as they come."

Willoughby paled.

"Did he do it?"

"Not yet," Yasha said. "We'd have heard if he had."

"He's got to be stopped," Willoughby said. "Who's running him?"

"The usual crowd. But Volkov doesn't take day-to-day orders.

Once he's given a job he goes underground, and he doesn't resurface until it's done."

"That's terrific," Willoughby said weakly. "Just wonderful. So where the fuck is Fairbrother?"

"God knows," Yasha said. "Somewhere in London, I believe. But I can promise you one thing: wherever Fairbrother is, Volkov cannot be far behind."

"So if I find Volkov," Willoughby reasoned, "I may be able to trace Fairbrother."

"Why not?" Yasha said. "Would it help if I gave you Volkov's photograph, and other information?"

"Would it help?" Willoughby cried. "You bet your Armenian ass it would."

Yasha nodded thoughtfully.

"Tricky," he mused. "This could get me into a lot of trouble. After all, I'd be disrupting a liquidation ordered at the highest level."

Willoughby looked upwards in exasperation.

"Okay, okay," he groaned. "What's the price?"

"I believe you said something about a Vax 8800 . . ."

"Up yours, Yasha," Willoughby snapped. "That item's right off the menu."

"Anything you say," Yasha smiled. "But it's the only way I could justify it to my superiors."

For a full minute, Willoughby sat perfectly still. Then, through gritted teeth, he said: "Okay, you little fuck. One Vax 8800. But I want everything you've got, including dental records and fingerprints."

"They're yours," Yasha said. "But I warn you, this man Volkov won't be easy to find. And if you succeed, he'll give you a hard time."

"Mean sonofabitch, huh?"

"Vicious. Possibly psychotic, too. But he's wonderfully efficient. They just send him out, and the job's as good as done. It may take weeks or even months, but he gets there in the end. You could say he was a human 'fire and forget' weapon."

Willoughby closed his eyes and drummed his fingers on the arm of his seat.

"You know something?" he said. "I've just about had enough of fire and forget weapons."

"What do you mean?"

Willoughby waved his hand.

"Forget it," he said. "Just forget it."

THIRTY-NINE

Dr Grant was puzzled. Despite Willoughby's claims to the contrary, he remained convinced that Professor Fairbrother was not a Soviet spy. He was sure that Fairbrother's disappearance was somehow related to the scientific article mentioned in the professor's diary. Exactly how the two were connected was a mystery to Dr Grant, but he felt obliged to try to find out.

So he went to the nearest library, and after half an hour's search, he unearthed the article in question. It lay in the back pages of a well-known scientific quarterly, among items of general interest. Strictly speaking, it was not a scientific article at all, but a philosophical one. It was entitled, "Can there ever be a ghost in the machine?" and it concerned Fairbrother's field of study, artificial intelligence.

The writer treated his subject with some scepticism. He did not believe it was possible to create an artificial brain—not a genuine one, at any rate. He conceded that one could build a machine which appeared to do everything a brain could. But, he said, such a machine would still not be a brain, because it would not contain a mind. It would lack thought, fears, desires, attitudes, and all the other things which made up consciousness. Seen from the outside, the artificial brain might give every appearance of having these things, but from the inside—from the brain's own viewpoint—there would be nothing.

It was a well-argued article, though Dr Grant was far from persuaded by it. But he understood why Clement Fairbrother would have taken it very seriously indeed. If the writer's conclusion was true, it undermined the very foundations of Fairbrother's work.

Dr Grant decided to speak to the article's author, who was a professor of philosophy at the University of Rome. According to the diary, Fairbrother had spoken to this man, though the details of their conversation were unrecorded. It was just possible that

Fairbrother had said something of importance to the philosopher, something which would help explain what had become of him.

Dr Grant phoned Rome's Faculty of Philosophy, and although it was evening in Italy, a helpful caretaker managed to find the Professor's home telephone number. Three minutes later, Dr Grant was speaking to the philosopher himself, an Englishman called Michael Wyman.

"I'm real sorry to disturb you this late," Dr Grant said, after introducing himself. "But it's extremely urgent, and I think you can help."

"Not to worry," Professor Wyman said genially. "I frequently receive late-night cries for help—they're usually from my students, the night before their exams. What can I do for you?"

Dr Grant recounted how Clement Fairbrother had gone missing, and how the journal discussed Wyman's paper.

"Yes indeed," Wyman said. "I've known Clem Fairbrother for years, you know. We were Fellows of the same college. Nice chap, though a little intense, even by Oxbridge standards."

"Looks like your article gave him a big headache."

"It jolly well did," Wyman agreed. "He phoned me about it and blabbered on for hours. The poor chap was desperate to prove me wrong, you see."

"But he couldn't?"

"Not with his style of argument. It was surprising, really: all his professional objectivity had gone straight through the window. He took it so awfully personally. Not the done thing in philosophy. Or science, as you must know."

"Sure," Dr Grant nodded. "What kind of things was he saying?"

"He said I *had* to be wrong. I said 'Why?' He said, 'Because if you're right, I've been practising a huge deception—both on my colleagues and myself.'"

"He used those words?" Dr Grant said excitedly. "Those exact words?"

"More or less," Wyman said. "Indeed, that was his whole response to my article. I hadn't just proved him a failure, apparently: I'd proved him a fraud as well. Quite preposterous, don't you think?"

"Yeah, but I can understand why he thought that."

"He enjoyed some success with his work, didn't he?" Wyman said.

"A hell of a lot," Dr Grant said. "More than most people thought possible."

The Englishman gave a knowing chuckle.

"That's always the way, isn't it?" he observed. "It's always the most respected and brilliant people who tear their hair out and call themselves failures. The mediocre chaps like me just sit back, relax, and accept our nonentity."

"Was Clem always like that?"

"Most definitely. He tore his hair out when he was a graduate student, and he's been doing the same ever since. By the time the poor fellow's completely bald, he should have a Nobel Prize."

"Let's hope so," Dr Grant said thoughtfully. "Anyway, many thanks for your help."

"Was any of that useful?" Wyman said, in surprise.

"It certainly was," Dr Grant said. "You've just cleared up a big question mark. Good-night, Professor."

"Cheerio."

Dr Grant put the phone down and clapped his hands in relief.

"I knew it!" he said.

He looked at his watch. It was too late to phone Willoughby now, but he would do so in the morning. Dr Grant's only regret was that he would not be able to see Willoughby's expression when he told him the news.

FORTY

Chief Superintendent Halliwell was a reasonable man. He was famed for his calmness and common sense. His colleagues at New Scotland Yard all agreed that he was a model of patience and courtesy. But right now, these qualities were all being put to some strain. In fact, Chief Superintendent Halliwell felt rather exasperated.

"It's two a.m., Mr Ximenez," he said. "Surely this could wait until the morning? A few more hours wouldn't make that much difference."

"If it could have waited, it would have waited," Ximenez said. "You heard what the ambassador said. We regard it as a major emergency."

Halliwell sniffed. His idea of a major emergency differed somewhat from the American ambassador's.

"I accept that this Russian—whassisname, Volvo?"

"Volkov."

"Yes, Volkov. I accept he's a potential danger. I'm not arguing with that."

"He's a paid assassin," Ximenez said.

"And he's trying to kill this Fairbrother bloke?"

"Right," Ximenez nodded.

"And Fairbrother is also on the run?"

"Right."

"So you're asking us to launch an immediate manhunt for Volkov?"

"Right."

"But not Fairbrother."

"Right."

Chief Superintendent Halliwell scratched the top of his head.

"It could just be the time of night," he said, "but this is where I get a bit lost. I mean, if it's Fairbrother you really want, why not put out an alert for him?"

"I explained this," Ximenez said. "Fairbrother's our problem. An internal matter. We want his name kept right out of this, see?"

"But why?" Halliwell demanded. "That's the part I don't get."

"Fairbrother was working for the US Department of Defense. He is in possession of highly sensitive information. Basically, Mr Halliwell, this guy is a walking file cabinet of state secrets. We want him, and everything to do with him, to be kept well out of the public eye. I'm sorry I can't be more specific."

"I'm sorry too," Halliwell said drily. "A little more information would make things run a lot smoother, you know."

Ximenez shrugged.

"It's a hard life," he said. "But I'll tell you what I can do. We've just received pictures of—my God, Al, you look like Flash Gordon."

Halliwell followed Ximenez's gaze, and saw a strange orange apparition in the doorway.

"Bloody hell," he muttered. "Who are you?"

"Your friendly neighbourhood space man," Willoughby said, as he lit a cigarette. "The guys at Mildenhall Air Base didn't give me time to change out of this. Did I hear you say something about pictures, Bill?"

"Yeah," Ximenez said. "The Russians sent them round half an hour ago. Looks like you've been busy."

Willoughby waved his cigarette nonchalantly.

"All part of the struggle for truth, justice and the American way. But listen, Mr—"

"Halliwell. Chief Superintendent."

"You gotta find this Volkov guy, fast as possible."

"So Mr Ximenez was saying. But on what grounds? You say he's planning to kill somebody, but you won't let us use that person's name. You're making it very difficult for us. Very difficult indeed."

"Relax, man," Willoughby said. "I'll make it real easy for you. This guy is wanted for over thirty political assassinations in Europe over the last twelve years. Interpol has a file on him the size of *War and Peace*. He's wanted in eight separate countries, under five different names—mostly Polish ones, because that's his usual cover. Now that helps, doesn't it?"

"It's a start," Halliwell said grudgingly.

"And I'll go one better," Willoughby offered. "We'll put up a fifty thousand pound reward for information leading to his arrest. Cash on the nail, no arguments. And if it's one of your people who grabs him, we'll drop an extra ten grand into your Police Benevolent Fund."

At once, Chief Superintendent Halliwell's humour improved.

"That's most generous of you," he said.

Ximenez gazed at his colleague uneasily.

"You got authorisation for this, Al?"

"No, Bill," Willoughby said wearily. "I'm just an eccentric millionaire. Okay, Mr Halliwell, this is what you do. You put out an APB—"

"A what?"

"Sorry, wrong country. You put out an alert to all your officers. You give the photos to all the newspapers, TV and radio stations, and tell them we've got a homicidal Polish maniac on the loose—"

"I do know how to do my job," Halliwell said.

"Yeah?" Willoughby grunted. "That makes you a very unusual Brit, Mr Halliwell. Anyway, we have to find Volkov by tomorrow night—sooner, if possible. You think you can do that?"

"I can't possibly give you any guarantees," Halliwell said. "For all we know, this Russian may be out of the country by now."

"He isn't," Willoughby said firmly. "He's in London, and he'll only leave when his work's finished. Trouble is, that could be very soon."

FORTY-ONE

Volkov, the pseudo-Pole, looked at his street map and nodded. As he had thought, he was standing in St George's Circus, a noisy traffic roundabout one mile south of the Thames. Despite the constant flow of cars, this was a curiously dead place, made up largely of broken pavements and grubby brick buildings of no discernible function. The road was lined by a weary grey row of trees, which fought a losing battle against the petrol fumes and dust. Beneath their branches, a couple of iron benches offered a morning gathering-place for a handful of derelicts.

Once again, Volkov took out the photograph of Fairbrother, and went up to the nearest vagrants, a pair of scrofulous old men who were sharing a bottle of cider.

"1963," said one of them. "Definitely."

"How can you be sure?" his friend asked.

"Because it was the year Kennedy got shot. That's how I know."

"Good memory you've got."

"Bloody good," the first man agreed. "But then, you don't forget your very last shag, do you?"

"Guess not. Why, that's nearly thirty years ago. You saying you haven't had your end away since Kennedy died?"

"I didn't plan it that way, you understand."

"'Course not," the second man said. "Just happens like that. Mine was—ooh, let me think. Before the Yom Kippur war, I know that."

"1972, wasn't it?"

"1973. I remember her, 'cause she had tattooed nipples. Never seen nothing like it."

"My friends," Volkov said. "Have you seen this man?"

He held out the photograph expectantly.

"Who's that?" the first man asked.

"A friend of mine I am seeking. Do you know him?"

"Looks just like my cousin Dan," the second man said. "Same nose, same silly grin."

"No," Volkov said firmly. "This is not Dan. This is Clement Fairbrother. Clem. Do you know his name?"

"I knew a Clem Bailey once," the first man said brightly.

"And I knew a Clem Smith," the second man added. "But he died. Pneumonia, I think it was."

"Nasty, that. But cancer's worse."

"Ooh, yes. A friend of mine got cancer in the stomach. Had to carry his crap around in a plastic bag. Didn't do him no good, though. He still died."

"Of the cancer?"

"No. In a car accident."

"This Clem is called Fairbrother," Volkov said. "He is alive, and maybe you have seen him. I am told he has three friends: a big Scotchman, an Englishman, and a punk rocker."

"That sounds like a joke," the first man smiled. "There was an Englishman, a Scotsman and a punk rocker . . ."

"They're Indians," the second man said.

"Who are?"

"Punks."

"Indians? They don't look like wogs to me. Got white skins, they have."

"Not wog Indians. Red Indians."

"You sure?"

"Positive. They're Mohicans, apparently. You can tell by their haircuts."

"Have you seen these four people?" Volkov said, his temper beginning to fray.

"You said there was three," the first man said accusingly.

"Four," Volkov barked. "Fairbrother and three friends."

The two old men frowned in concentration.

"Wait a minute . . ." the first man said.

"Last night, at the Bin."

"Yeah, there was four there, wasn't there?"

"Let's see that photo again."

They took another look at Fairbrother's picture, and nodded.

"It was him, definitely."

"Staying in your hostel?" Volkov said eagerly.

"Yeah. The Bin, we call it."

"Where is this Bin?"

"Off Blackfriars Road. Go up there, hundred yards, turn right. Tall yellow house."

"Many, many thanks, my friends," Volkov said heartily. "I shall go there now."

"No point," the first man said.

"No?"

"What time is it?"

Volkov looked at his watch.

"Eleven and thirty."

"You're too late, then."

"It's shut during the day," the second man explained. "Closed two hours ago. You should come back at seven tonight. Your mates'll be there."

"How can you be sure?" Volkov asked.

"'Cause you have to pay for three nights. They won't let you stay for just one. Now, your mates only turned up last night, so they're bound to come tonight, aren't they?"

"Of course," Volkov said. "I shall see them then. Many thanks again, my friends."

"Pleasure," the first man replied. "Now, what was you saying about them tatooed nipples?"

FORTY-TWO

Willoughby angrily snatched up the phone. This was no time for interruptions.

"Yeah?" he snarled.

"Willoughby? This is Dr Grant. I've got news for you."

"I hope it's good, Doc," Willoughby said. "Because all I'm getting at the moment is a crock of shit."

"Remember the article which upset Fairbrother so much?"

"What about it?"

"It was about his work. A theoretical piece. To put it crudely, the writer tried to prove Fairbrother's work was a waste of time. He said you could never build a brain, the way Fairbrother hoped he could."

"Big deal," Willoughby said. "Who gives a screw?"

"Fairbrother did. He couldn't disprove the argument. It made him so mad he even phoned the writer about it."

"Doc," Willoughby said evenly, "I'm sure this is all good gossip for your out-of-term science conferences, along with who's balling whom, and Professor Schmockstein's latest theory of the universe. But right now I am a very busy man, and—"

"Just *listen*, will you?" Dr Grant shrieked. "I spoke to this writer last night. Fairbrother didn't just chew the guy's ear off. He said that if the article was right, he himself had been, quote, 'practising a huge deception on himself and his colleagues,' unquote."

Willoughby gave a startled blink.

"He said that?"

"Those very words," Dr Grant said. "And it makes sense, too. I've checked back, and it all ties in perfectly."

"Okay," Willoughby nodded. "Thanks for telling me."

"How's it going at your end?" Dr Grant enquired.

"Don't ask," Willoughby sighed. "See you round, Doc."

He put the phone down, and looked up at Semple and Naylor,

who were sitting before his desk like a pair of schoolboys waiting to be flogged.

"Right you chisellers," he said grimly. "I've got it all now. So let's recap. You burgled Fairbrother's house. Why?"

"As we told you the first time," Semple said, "it really was routine."

"You burgle all your own scientists' homes?" Willoughby said incredulously.

"Not all," Naylor said.

"Just the likely ones," Semple explained.

"Likely to do what?" Willoughby said. "Never mind, we'll get to that later. So when you burgled Fairbrother, you found his diary. And you thought you'd hit the jackpot, right?"

"No thought about it," Naylor grinned. "It was all there."

"A full confession."

"He'd defrauded his people."

"Bad boy."

"Naughty."

"So you decided to blackmail him," Willoughby said. "To use him for a sting on the Russians."

"Exactly," Semple said. "And a jolly good idea it was too."

"A whizzo wheeze," Naylor concurred.

"Even if we say so ourselves."

"It figures," Willoughby said thoughtfully. "MI5 is short of cash, so what better way to fill your purse than by screwing Yasha?"

"Absolutely," Semple nodded eagerly.

"Couldn't happen to a nicer chap," Naylor observed.

"Not just that," Willoughby said, "but you were also doing your bit to keep the Cold War alive. Because that's your real problem, isn't it?"

Semple looked up at the ceiling. Naylor examined his shoes.

"Not quite with you, old man," Semple muttered.

"Rather opaque," Naylor mused.

"You know exactly what I mean," Willoughby insisted. "You said it yourselves. Ever since the Russians started cleaning up their act, you guys have been on the defensive. Your workload's drying up, your budgets are getting slashed, and you're running out of things to do. That's why you're dreaming up these smart-assed schemes. That's why you're checking up on all these scientists. You're trying to look busy."

"Now steady on, old boy," Semple protested.

"I wouldn't go quite that far," Naylor said.

"You not only would, man, you did. The Russians have got a word for what you guys have been up to. They call it *pokazukha*."

"Poker what?"

"It means boasting about phony achievements. That's what all this is about. Inventing nice entries for your résumé."

"Nothing wrong with that," Semple pouted.

"Keeps the ball rolling," Naylor argued.

"Keeps things on the boil. And besides, we weren't hurting anybody. No innocent bystanders, are there?"

"No?" Willoughby said. "What about Fairbrother?"

"What about him?" Semple said. "He did the job, and there were no hitches. We even offered him a cut of the takings, but the silly oik refused."

"Inexplicable," Naylor said. "And when we asked him to do one more job, he simply vanished on us."

"Poor bastard," Willoughby groaned.

"Oh, rot," Semple snorted. "He's an old rogue. Diddled your people for years. He admitted it himself."

"That's just where you're wrong," Willoughby said. "I read that entry in his diary. I thought he was confessing to being a spy. You thought he was confessing to defrauding our government. We were both mistaken."

The MI5 men sat bolt upright.

"What?"

"He meant something else," Willoughby said. "The poor sonofabitch just thought his work was no good. He thought he'd been wrong for years. He thought he conned everybody, *including himself*. That's why he got depressed. That's why he came back to England."

"Oh Lord," Semple exclaimed.

"Gosh," Naylor said. "That's—"

"That's awful."

"Dreadful."

"Ghastly."

"More than you know," Willoughby said.

He picked up that afternoon's edition of the *Evening Standard* and waved the front page at the MI5 men. It showed a large photograph of an unpleasant-looking gentleman, under the head-line MAD KILLER: £50,000 REWARD OFFERED.

"See this guy?" Willoughby said. "After you blackmailed Fairbrother into stinging the KGB, the Russians got very angry. They sent this gorilla out to punish Fairbrother."

"Oh dear," Naylor winced.

"And if he finds Fairbrother before we do," Willoughby said, "I'll hold you mothers personally responsible. Not just for the murder, but for the international disaster that follows. Now beat it."

FORTY-THREE

Cosmonaut Grigovin breathed in deeply, and flung the chest expander apart. He counted to ten and let go, exhaling with a sound like a slashed tyre. He repeated the action twenty times, taking a little longer over each pull. At the other end of the Salyut, Rogov was performing a series of isometric exercises. It was all part of the daily routine in space.

"Did I tell you about the car?" Grigovin said.

"No," Rogov said, as he crushed the palms of his hands together with all his strength.

"On top of everything else, my wife wants a Western car."

"Does she, indeed?" Rogov laughed. "And where are you supposed to find one of those?"

"The same place I'm supposed to find the compact disc player," Grigovin said. "The big mythical storehouse labelled 'Cosmonaut's Privileges'."

He threw the chest expander over his back, and began a series of sharp forward pulls.

"My cousin Igor was in England last year," Rogov said. "He told me about the kind of cars they drive there."

"Very nice, I hear."

"Oh yes. The real status symbol is something called a Yuppy."

"A what?"

"It's a German sports car," Rogov explained. "Supposed to be very popular among the young mercantile classes."

"I've heard about those people," Grigovin nodded. "They make a cult out of being young, rich and selfish. There's a nickname for them isn't there?"

"That's right," Rogov said. "They're known as Porsches."

Suddenly, the main radio let out a high-pitched shriek. Grigovin let his chest expander float away, and he went over to the control console.

"What the devil's that?" he frowned. "Some kind of interference, but—"

"The panels!" Grigovin shouted. "They're moving."

The Salyut rocked as an unseen force swivelled its large solar panels back and forth. On Grigovin's console, the display of counters gave a series of random flashes, and all the meter needles flickered wildly from side to side.

"It's coming from outside," Grigovin said. "These are all external commands. Hold on."

He turned off the radio circuits, disconnecting the outside antennas which received pre-programmed commands from the computers on earth. Then he turned on the internal controls. At once the solar panels stopped swaying, and the meter needles subsided.

"Must be a computer hitch downstairs," Rogov reasoned. "Some kind of bug in the software."

"On automatic control? Come off it, Sergei. We weren't doing anything out of the ordinary. The computers were just supposed to keep us still."

"A solar flare, then," Rogov suggested. "They can play havoc with the systems. I'll take a look."

He went over to the nearest porthole, and peered out towards the sun. There were no obvious cosmic disturbances, but these things were not always visible to the naked eye. Just as Rogov was about to turn away, he noticed something over to his far left.

"Oleg," he said. "Look in the telescope. I think it's the American satellite. Port side, about three hundred feet away."

Grigovin moved down to the telescope compartment as quickly as his weightlessness allowed. He switched on the cameras, and searched through space until he found what he wanted.

"You're right," he said. "Look on the radar, will you? What do you see?"

Rogov glanced at the bright green screen and frowned.

"Nothing," he said. "Not even the hint of a blip."

"The satellite's jamming it," Grigovin said. "And if she's doing that, she must also be jamming our radio."

"The damned thing is trying to spoof us," Rogov said, aghast. "She's trying to bring us down. For heaven's sake, Oleg—"

"Relax, Sergei," Grigovin said. "She's slightly further away now. I think she's reached the apogee of her orbit. Try the radio again."

Rogov turned on the loudspeaker, and was greeted by the same ear-shattering noise. But the sound was appreciably fainter than before, and it grew weaker by the second. Rogov turned off the radio and let out a gasp of relief.

"Five minutes and she'll be gone," he said. "But have you noticed, she's getting closer with every sweep? Next time, she'll be right up our arses. Then what?"

"Then nothing," Grigovin said confidently. "She had no joy this time, did she? She tried to spoof us, and we just went manual. She's an ASAT weapon, remember. She's not built to tackle human beings."

"You're forgetting something," Rogov said. "She has cannons."

Rogov paled.

"We've got to get out of here," he whispered.

He joined Rogov at the radio and turned it on once more. The interference was still there, but he now could make out the anxious voices at Mission Control.

". . . to Salyut. Baikonur to Salyut. Please confirm if you are receiving, over."

"It's all right," Grigovin said. "We're here."

"Where the hell have you been? And what's that noise?"

"The American satellite," Grigovin said, and he recounted what had happened.

"Are you absolutely sure it was the American?" Mission Control demanded.

"Positive," Rogov said. "And you people had better do something about it."

There was a crackle at the other end, and another voice joined the conversation.

"This is Kamenev. You'll have to come down from there, my children. How soon can you do it?"

"Ages," Grigovin said. "If we started work now, we'd need about thirteen hours to prepare the docking module and seal it off. Then we'd have to realign the craft and wait until the right part of the orbit. At a rough guess, that's another eight hours."

There was a pause as Kamenev made his own calculations. The cosmonauts could hear him puffing frantically on his cigar.

"It's too late, my children," he concluded. "The American satellite will be back by then."

"What do we do?" Rogov howled. "I'm a married man, Professor. I have dependents."

"Shut up, Sergei," Grigovin hissed.

"The satellite selects its targets by camera," Kamenev said. "At least, we think it does. But all its weaponry depends chiefly on infra-red scanners. So the first thing you must do is reduce your infra-red signature to a minimum. Change it, if possible."

"And how do we do that?"

"The chief target must be the solar panels," Kamenev said. "When the satellite comes into sight, tilt your panels away from the sun, my children, so that no light is reflected."

"I understand," Grigovin said.

"Also, black out your portholes. Don't let any light escape through the glass. How much internal power do you have left?"

"The batteries are good for another ten days."

"Good. And the hydrazine?"

"There's enough to fire the docking capsule away for our escape."

"Excellent, excellent. What about the Salyut's own propulsion system?"

"Not much there," Rogov said. "Enough for a few small realignments, but little more than that."

"How about a jettison?" Kamenev said.

"No," Grigovin said, shaking his head. "At least, not a full one."

"A partial one may be all you need," Kamenev said thoughtfully. "Very well, my children, I have an idea. It's crude and risky, but I don't think you have any alternative. Listen carefully . . ."

FORTY-FOUR

It was eight p.m. as Volkov arrived at the hostel off Blackfriars Road. The entrance lobby was narrow and gloomy, and it was steeped in the familiar aroma of sweat, urine and despondency. Volkov's boots kicked up clouds of dust from the carpet as he stepped inside. Beneath the dull glow of a forty-watt bulb, a bearded young man sat at the reception desk, reading a Christian magazine.

"Good-evening my friend," Volkov said cheerfully.

"Hi," said the young man. "I'm afraid we're full tonight. If you like, I can—"

"Not to worry. I am not here for a bed. I am looking for a friend."

"A friend?" the young man repeated. "Someone here, you mean?"

"Yes, yes," Volkov nodded. "I would like to look inside, please."

"I'm very sorry," the young man said. "But that's against the rules. We don't allow residents to bring in guests."

"No?" Volkov frowned. "Why not?"

The young man gave an embarrassed grin.

"It can lead to problems, you see."

"What problems?"

"Ah, well," the young man stammered. "You see, some people bring back the wrong kind of friends."

Volkov shook his head in perplexity.

"What you talking about, my friend?"

The young man swallowed a few times, and looked away.

"Well, sometimes," he said, "men bring in, you know, women."

Volkov threw his head back and roared with laughter.

"You mean they fuck?" he bellowed. "That is what you are saying, yes? Fucky-fuck?"

The young man closed his eyes and shuddered.

"That sort of thing," he said.

"Fucky-fuck is not allowed, eh?" Volkov grinned.

"Not here, at any rate."

"You the boss, my friend," Volkov shrugged. "But that is all right. I want to see a man."

"I'm sure," the young man gasped. "But that's not allowed either, I'm afraid."

"What?" Volkov said. "What you think I am?"

He leaned over the desk and pointed a truculent finger at the young man's nose.

"You think I fuck man?" he demanded. "You saying I am—"

"Oh gosh, no," the young man said hastily. "Nothing of the sort. It's just that all guests—of whatever kind—aren't allowed."

"But I have to see my friend," Volkov insisted. "My good old friend inside."

"Can't it wait until the morning?"

"No! This is urgent news I have for him. I must see him now."

"Oh dear," the young man said. "Well, perhaps I could ask him to come out here. Would that do?"

Volkov thought about this, then threw up his hands.

"Yes, okay, my friend. I will see him here."

"And who is this gentleman?"

"His name is Fairbrother. Clement Fairbrother."

The young man reached for his guest-list, and paused.

"Is he with three other people?" he asked. "A large Scottish gentleman, and—"

"Yes, yes," Volkov said eagerly. "That is the man."

"Oh gosh," the young man said. "I'm terribly sorry, but they're not here."

"No? Not here yet?"

"They've been here all right. But I'm afraid we had to send them away."

Volkov's eyes popped.

"Why?" he shouted. "Why you do this? You crazy or something?"

"I'm afraid the Scottish gentleman was intoxicated," the young man said stiffly. "And so was the older companion. Now the rules are quite clear about this: we don't allow drinking, and we won't admit intoxicated people."

"But Fairbrother, he was drunk?"

"No," the young man admitted. "He wasn't. But when we sent away the two intoxicated gentlemen, your Mr Fairbrother decided to go with them. So did the other young man."

"Where?" Volkov said quickly. "Where they go?"

"I'm sorry, I've no idea."

"Some other place near here?"

"Possibly," the young man said. "But I doubt if they'll find any beds. Most places are full up by seven, you see—"

He was interrupted by a torrent of oaths from Volkov. Most of the abuse was in Russian, but the young man grasped the general idea. Finally, when Volkov had calmed down a little, his invective reverted to something resembling English.

"You fuck bloody fool! You fuck shit-face! Just because one man drinks too much, you throw him out. Incredible! How can you do this, you shit? Where I come from, everyone drink too much. Where I come from, if you threw all drinkers out into the street, nobody left inside!"

"My word," said the young man. "I'm sorry to hear that. Oh no, please—"

Volkov grabbed the young man by the beard, and lifted him to his feet.

"I had this man Fairbrother," he growled. "I had him here. But you lose him from me, you stupid prick! Now where I find him, eh? You tell me this, shit!"

"Ah, I might be able to help there," the young man whimpered. "Please don't hit me—"

"You tell me where he is," Volkov said, "or I hit you so hard your face will come out with your shit."

"He'll be here tomorrow," the young man said. "He has to be. He's got one night left. They all have. They've paid for three nights, you see—"

"You sure?"

"Positive. It's the rules."

Volkov let go of the beard, and tossed the young man back into his seat.

"Rules," he snorted. "I shit on your fuck bloody rules. Tomorrow night, then. And if you are lying . . ."

He waved his fist, and left the rest to the young man's imagination.

FORTY-FIVE

Had Volkov but known it, he could have found his quarry just two hundred yards away. After their eviction from the hostel, the four friends had tried the other shelters around St George's Circus, though with no success. But instead of returning to Cardboard City, they decided to try their hands at "skippering"—moving into a derelict building for the night.

Fortunately, there was no shortage of likely premises in the area, and after a twenty minute search they found precisely what they wanted: a condemned five-storey house in Borough Road. There was little left of the place apart from its roof and outer walls; the inside was a burned-out shell, knee-high in rubble and the remains of other nocturnal visitations. But it was quiet and safe from the attention of passing policemen, so the friends were content to make themselves at home there. They formed a circle in the darkness, lit rolled-up cigarettes, and shared out a bottle of sherry.

"Listen Clem," Spider said. "I've been thinking about what you were saying at the church hall. About making a brain—"

"Oh, pack it in," Craig groaned. "We've had enough of that."

"I just want to know," Spider persisted. "Seriously: why would anyone want to do it?"

"Do what, exactly?" Clem asked.

"You know. Build a brain."

"Because if you built one," Clem said, "you'd know more about how our own brains work. And once you knew that, you could make brains that were even better than ours."

"That shouldn't be too hard," Miles observed. "Don't know about your brain, old boy, but mine's a disaster area nowadays."

"At the moment," Clem went on, "machines are stupid. Clumsy. Naïve. But if they had artificial brains, they could—"

"Chuck even more of us on the scrapheap," Craig grunted.

"That's right," Miles agreed. "Quite a few of our crowd are victims of new technology. Ever thought about that, Clem old boy?"

"Of course I have," Clem said. "But . . . Well, for every job it destroys, it makes ten more new ones."

"You don't sound convinced," Miles said. "And I don't blame you. I admit I've sacked a few people in my time. But I bet you sacked far more."

"Wait a minute," Spider said. "You said you worked for the American military, Clem."

"That's right."

"Then those intelligent machines you built, they're smart weapons, aren't they?"

"Some were," Clem nodded. "The so-called fire and forget technology."

"Sounds like most bosses I've worked for," Craig observed. "The bastards fire you and forget you."

"That's not what it means," Spider said impatiently. "Fire and forget is—"

He was interrupted by a fit of coughing from Miles. As usual, the others waited for the attack to subside before trying to resume their conversation. But this time, the coughing did not stop; it grew louder and more violent.

"You okay, Miles?" Craig muttered.

Miles did not reply. He slumped forward and retched, and though the others could not see him, they heard the thick liquid slopping on to the floor.

"It's a bad one this time," Spider said.

Clem struck a match, and grimaced.

"Blood again," he said. "I'm sorry Miles, but we'll have to get you to a doctor."

"Guy's Hospital isn't far," Spider said. "About ten minutes' walk."

"Very well," Clem decided. "We'll take him there. Come on, Miles. On your feet."

Miles tried to stand, but his convulsions were too severe. He fell back on to his knees and continued to throw up.

"I'll carry him," Craig said.

"Want a hand?" Spider offered.

"Bugger that," Craig grunted. "Just watch me."

With no apparent effort, the big Scotsman picked Miles up and threw him over his shoulder in a fireman's lift.

"Well done," Clem said, and they left the building.

The friends staggered up the road, and turned left into Borough High Street. The journey took a little longer than expected, thanks to Miles' savage attacks of nausea. But after two or three bouts, they decided to press on at full speed and let Miles regurgitate en route. The patient clung on to Craig's waist, and left a long snail-like trail of vomit all the way to the hospital.

When they arrived at the casualty department, the duty nurse asked them to wait at the end of a long queue. But one more liquid explosion persuaded her of the urgency of Miles' condition. He was whisked away to a side-ward, while his three friends sat in the waiting room.

"Do you think he'll be okay?" Spider asked anxiously.

"I hope so," Clem said.

"Poor old bugger," Craig sighed. "Still, there's nothing much we can do now. Hey, do you think we can get a cup of tea here? Oy, you, lady: do they do tea here?"

The lady, like most other people in the waiting room, was gazing at the ragged friends in horrified fascination. But when Craig spoke to her, she turned her head away in embarrassment.

"What about you, mate?" Craig said to the man beside her. "Seen a tea trolley or something?"

The man looked down at his lap.

"We're not bloody animals, you know," Spider said indignantly. "You can talk to us."

"I doubt it," Clem said drily.

Spider hissed angrily, and picked up a newspaper someone had left in the next seat.

"Fifty thousand pound reward," he read. "I could use that. Hang on a minute . . ."

He showed the front page to his friends.

"I've seen him," he said. "I don't know where, but I've definitely seen this feller."

"Pretty face, hasn't he?" Clem observed.

"He's new to me," Craig said. "I wouldn't forget a face like that."

"I remember now," Spider said. "You know I was trying to get work the other day at a hotel kitchen? Well, this feller was in the queue. A big bastard—big as you are, Craig."

"Did he get the job?" Clem said. "If he did, you might be able to—"

"No," Spider said. "He got turned away with the rest of us."

"You think he's a dosser, like us?" Craig said.

"Has to be. Hello, I think we're wanted."

A tired young doctor emerged from the side-ward, and a nurse pointed him towards the three Cardboard Citizens.

"Good-evening," he said. "I think you should know we intend to keep your friend here a while. So if you don't feel like waiting, you can come back later."

"Tomorrow?" Clem said.

"No, just a couple of hours. I'm pretty sure what the problem is, but I need to confirm it with some tests."

"Is it serious?" Spider asked.

The doctor shrugged.

"It doesn't have to be," he said. "Your friend is suffering from acute gastritis. He may well have a gastric ulcer, too, but we'll have to X-ray him to find out."

"Why doesn't it have to be serious?" Clem asked.

"The problem is entirely of your friend's making. He drinks too much. If he stopped, so would the vomiting, and the ulcer would probably clear up too."

"Big 'if'," Craig chuckled.

"I know," the doctor sighed. "Pretty useless asking you guys to pack in the booze, isn't it? But that's what's needed."

"What can you do for him?" Spider asked.

"Not much. A few pills and a warning. It's not serious enough to warrant surgery—yet."

"But . . . ?"

"But if he has an ulcer, it might perforate. One more drinking bout could do it. And then, anything might happen."

"You mean he could die?" Clem said.

"It's always a possibility," the doctor nodded. "I told him this, but I was wasting my breath, wasn't I? The way you people live

176

... Why do you do it? I mean, I know it's hard for you. But for heaven's sake, why make it worse for yourselves?"

"It's quite illogical," Clem agreed. "Doesn't make any sense at all. But you see, Doctor, I have recently made an important discovery: the brain is a highly illogical instrument."

FORTY-SIX

Mr Linus C Mittelschuster IV was not pleased. It was four in the morning, and his nocturnal arrangements had been severely disrupted.

Mr Mittelschuster's wife, a formidable sixteen-stone lady with the handshake of an all-in wrestler, had flown to Paris for her monthly shopping trip. This gave Mr Mittelschuster an excellent opportunity to further his acquaintance with a pneumatic young lady in his embassy's trade section. By one a.m. their friendship had quite literally improved by leaps and bounds.

Unfortunately, Mr Mittelschuster was no longer a young man. Nowadays it took him at least three attempts before he could, as he quaintly put it, "oil the goddamn piston and work up a good head of steam". He was just about to embark on the fourth bout of mechanical engineering when he received a surprise call from the Soviet Foreign Ministry, demanding his immediate appearance on a matter of great urgency.

So with the deepest regret, Mr Mittelschuster left his young friend and presented himself in Mr Bryusov's office. He did not have the slightest idea of why he was wanted, but it was clear from the Foreign Minister's expression that the matter was indeed serious.

"I am so sorry to disturb you at this late hour," Bryusov said. "I trust it has not caused you too great an inconvenience."

"Nothing I can't finish later," Mr Mittelschuster shrugged. "At least, I damn well hope so."

"Good," Bryusov nodded. "Now, I would be grateful if you could tell me exactly what progress your country is making towards disabling the renegade satellite."

"The satellite?" Mr Mittelschuster blinked. "Is that what it's about?"

"Yes. We have been following your efforts as best we can, but we have seen little sign of success."

Mr Mittelschuster scratched his head.

"Well, Mr Bryusov, sir, I can't give you much detailed information right here and now, you understand. But I can tell you our people are doing all they can. 'Course, it may be a little while before they actually—"

"How long?" Bryusov demanded.

Mr Mittelschuster waved his hands helplessly.

"I just can't say, Mr Bryusov. We don't have any rigid timetable here. But I can't understand why you're so fired up about this, all of a sudden. Is our bird gunning for some fancy new Rooshian platform?"

"Not exactly," Bryusov said. "But it would seem that the next target is a Salyut space station."

Mr Mittelschuster grimaced. He had wondered how soon the Soviets would find out about that.

"Is . . . is that a fact?" he muttered. "Well, I'm real sorry to hear it, sir. But I thought it was understood there might be more damage to your country's space hardware. We didn't give you any bull about that, sir."

"We took that to mean satellites, Mr Mittelschuster."

"I never said that," Mr Mittelschuster retorted. "I just used the term 'space hardware'."

"Really, Mr Mittelschuster," Bryusov said reproachfully. "Do I have to explain that this is much more serious than an attack on our satellites? Do I?"

"No," Mr Mittelschuster conceded. "You don't. But fair's fair, Mr Bryusov. Our agreement covers all kinds of space hardware, and we've agreed to reimburse you in full."

"It is not merely a question of money," Bryusov said. "There is far more at stake here than—"

"Yeah, sure. I can see how your national pride would get kinda dented if we took out your space station. But rest assured, Mr Bryusov, sir: we promise not to tell anyone about it."

Bryusov's jaw fell.

"You won't—tell?" he breathed.

"Cross my heart and hope to die," Mr Mittelschuster grinned. "And look on the bright side. From what I hear, them Salyut stations are pretty clapped out. With the money we give you, you'll be able to build a whole new station. Why, it's just like a car insurance scam, only legal. We trash your old model, you get a shiny new one. Can't say fairer than that, can you, sir?"

Bryusov slapped his own ears, as if unable to believe what he was hearing.

"A car insurance scam," he repeated. "This is a regular occurrence in the United States?"

"I'll say," Mr Mittelschuster chuckled.

"And what about the car drivers?" Bryusov said. "You kill them too, for the insurance?"

"Eh?"

"Mr Mittelschuster," Bryusov said, "what are we supposed to do about the cosmonauts?"

Mr Mittelschuster began to understand. His face peeled open in a wide, ghastly grin.

"You . . . you telling me that Salyut's manned?"

"Yes, Mr Mittelschuster."

"You got people up there?"

"Yes, Mr Mittelschuster."

"Sweet Mother of Jesus," Mr Mittelschuster cried. "We never knew—"

"You know now," Bryusov snapped. "And I have a warning for you. Hitherto, the Foreign Ministry has, as you would say, kept the lid on this matter. We have followed the path of maximum discretion."

"You sure have," Mr Mittelschuster nodded. "And we do appreciate that, Mr Bryusov, sir."

"But there are other forces," Bryusov continued, "who take a different view of how the crisis should be handled. A radically different view."

"The military, huh?"

Bryusov spread his hands.

"So far," he said, "those forces have gone unheeded. But in the Soviet Union, cosmonauts are national heroes. If any should perish at the hands of your killer satellite, those other forces will get a new hearing. Do I make myself plain?"

"You bet," Mr Mittelschuster said. "Okay, Mr Bryusov, sir. We hear you loud and clear."

"I hope so," Bryusov said soberly. "For all our sakes."

FORTY-SEVEN

"How many sightings?" Willoughby said.

"About six hundred," said Chief Superintendent Halliwell. "Some may even be genuine."

It was eleven in the morning, and they were standing in an incident room at New Scotland Yard, from where Halliwell was conducting the search for Volkov. A team of twenty men and women sat at a bank of telephones, taking calls from the members of the public who were doubtless eager to lay their hands on the fifty thousand pound reward. Each call was logged on a slip of green paper, and added to a growing pile at the end of the room. Halliwell flicked casually through these reports, and nodded.

"About one in twenty is real, I'd say."

"How can you tell?" Willoughby asked.

"There's a pattern emerging," Halliwell said. "A number of the sightings were in or around hostels for homeless people. Others were on the Embankment, or the South Bank—all tramps' haunts."

"So he's posing as a hobo?"

"Looks like it. But he's got a reason. We got a call from one of the staff at St Benedict's hostel. The man claimed Volkov was looking for a friend, and he was waving a photograph around."

"Fairbrother?"

"Possibly," Halliwell said.

"So Fairbrother's a down-and-out," Willoughby said. "Jesus! No wonder we couldn't find him. There must be thousands of those guys in London."

"Around seventy-five thousand, at the last count," Halliwell said. "They're spread out all over the city, but there are a few major gathering-places. We're trying all of them, of course, but—"

"But what?" Willoughby said.

"If it's Fairbrother you really want," Halliwell said, "why

don't you let us search for him? We'll keep looking for Volkov, of course. But even if we find him, you've no guarantee that Fairbrother will be close by."

"I know, man, I know," Willoughby groaned. "You think I like doing it this way? It's crazy, but I've got no choice. My people won't let me break security on Fairbrother's name."

One of Halliwell's staff came up and handed the Chief Superintendent a note.

"This is for you," Halliwell said. "Your people are trying to track you down. There's a phone in the next office."

"Thanks," Willoughby said, and went to make his call. The number, he noted, was that of CIA Headquarters at Langley. There was no extension, simply the word "Sulphur", which Willoughby knew to be the Director's own line. He dialled the number, read out the extension name and his own, and waited until the Director's voice came through.

"You on scramble, Willoughby?"

"Sorry, no. What's happening?"

"Too much. Our little toy upstairs has started partying, and the Bears know all about it."

"Ouch," Willoughby said.

"It gets worse. Apparently there are two live Bears up there."

Willoughby let out a long, low whistle.

"But the Doc said—"

"As usual, Grant was talking through his butt," the CIA Director said bitterly. "He's down at Sunnyvale, trying to stop it all happening."

"And getting nowhere, huh?"

"Right. Which means we need your man as badly as ever. Where is he?"

"Somewhere in London. You know about the Bear on his tail? We should have him soon. We hope."

"Yeah, but what about the man himself?"

"If we get the Bear, we may get him. I repeat, may."

"That isn't good enough, Willoughby."

"I know it isn't. What do you expect? It's this stupid blackout you've put on our man's name. It screws up everything."

The CIA Director thought about this for a few moments, then sighed.

"Okay," he decided. "Release your man's name and picture. But tell the cops to be discreet: no publicity, no theatrics—"

"Trust me," Willoughby said, and he threw the phone down.

He fumbled in his pockets, until he found a passport photograph of Clem Fairbrother. Then he ran back into the incident room.

"Okay, Mr Halliwell," he announced. "There's been a change of policy."

FORTY-EIGHT

"She's getting closer," Rogov announced. "Look!"

"Relax," Grigovin said. "She's miles away."

"But it's fast, Oleg."

"We've still got a few minutes. Now strap yourself in, will you?"

They took their places at the aft end of the space station, inside the Soyuz capsule. Grigovin closed the docking hatch linking them to the Salyut station, and the two cosmonauts attached their suits to the capsule's life-support system. They were not yet able to leave for home: the preparations were far from complete. But if Kamenev's plan succeeded, it might buy them the necessary time.

At the opposite end of the space station, the Prospect service module had been emptied of its gear and sealed off. All its main connecting bolts were loosened, so it was now only held on to the main body of the Salyut by two detachable hydraulic lines and six electrical cables. The latter led back to the console in the Soyuz module, where Grigovin had transferred all the main controls.

"Ready?" Grigovin asked.

"Yes," Rogov said.

Grigovin turned on the radio headsets.

"Salyut to Mission Control," he said. "We're locked in, now."

"Splendid," Kamenev said. "Have you seen the American satellite?"

"Yes. She came into view about forty-five minutes ago."

"In that case," Kamenev said, "you have approximately seven minutes to go. I suggest you spend them on a final circuit-check. Better safe than sorry, my children."

"Right, Professor," Grigovin agreed. "Power circuit one working."

"Power one working, check," Rogov said.

"LSS circuit one working."

"LSS one, check . . ."

Down at Mission Control, Kamenev dabbed a handkerchief across his forehead, and turned to Marshal Zhdanov.

"The circuit check's not really necessary," he admitted. "But it's a kind of mantra, and it should take their minds off the danger."

"What are their chances?" Zhdanov asked. "Realistically."

"Six to four against," Kamenev said. "But it's the best thing I could think of."

Zhdanov nodded.

"I'm sure it is," he said. "And whatever the outcome, I'm grateful for your efforts, Comrade Kamenev. Thank you."

The Marshal, Kamenev noted, was surprisingly subdued. He had shed his bombast and ill-temper, and was standing calmly beside the professor as the Mission Control team performed its tasks. Then Kamenev understood: the Marshal was a soldier, and his histrionics were reserved for the frustrations of peace-time. Now he was at war, if only with a faraway electronic enemy. For the first time, Zhdanov was behaving as if he and Kamenev were on the same side.

"If only they were armed," Zhdanov muttered. "If only they could fight back . . ."

"It's too late for that," Kamenev said. "Just hope that this plan works."

"I tell you, Kamenev," Zhdanov whispered. "If one hair of my boys' heads is touched, I'll make those Americans pay. I'll make the fucking sky cave in. I don't care what Bryusov and the other pansies say. The military have some rights too, even in these crummy liberal times."

He said it slowly, and with none of his customary thunder. For that very reason, Kamenev found him doubly frightening.

Up in the frozen gloom, oblivious to the rage and fear of men, Fats glided swiftly towards its prey. Its orbit would bring it within a hundred feet of the Salyut, and at that range Fats could not possibly miss. As usual, Fats was aiming for its target's weakest spot—the fuel tanks. According to Fats' data banks, there were several to choose from: one in the Soyuz docking module, two smaller ones feeding the retro rockets in the centre of the space ship, and another pair further along, which served the Salyut's intermediate propulsion system.

But the biggest tank was at the far aft end, inside the Prospect service module. The Prospect did not just store ancillary equipment: its rockets provided the main navigational thrust for the entire Salyut system. Its tanks would therefore carry the greatest amount of fuel, and make the biggest explosion when hit. Fats locked its sights on to the centre of the Prospect capsule, and began a countdown from fifty.

"Here she comes," Grigovin said. "What are you doing, Sergei?"

"Praying," Rogov said. "And I suggest you do the same."

Grigovin shook his head in disgust, and watched Fats looming up on his console's video display.

"One hundred and twenty feet," he said. "One hundred . . . eighty . . . Now!"

He threw his switches, and the Prospect's rockets flared into life. At the same time, the central retro rockets fired, drawing the Salyut away from the Prospect module. Grigovin released the hydraulic arms, which gave the Prospect one last shove away from its mother craft, before dangling uselessly in space.

Then Fats fired. Its shells streaked towards the Prospect like Roman candles, and tore into the metal plate. For a millionth of a second the Prospect blew out into a dazzling orange ball, ringed by a spray of flaming shards. Then the light vanished, snuffed out at once by the black vacuum all around. All that remained were thousands of carbonised fragments, scattered in all directions like burnt confetti. And forty feet away hung the main body of the Salyut, charred, split and dented, like a tin can fished out of a bonfire.

Fats drew away from the devastation, gliding back along its orbital tram line for mile after mile, watching and listening for lingering signs of life. But there was nothing to see, and nothing to hear. All was silence, and Fats was soon out of sight on the other side of the globe.

"Salyut, this is Kamenev. Are you with us, my children? She's way out of range now. It's safe to talk."

"We're here, Professor," Grigovin said. "It seems—"

His next words were drowned out by the cries at Mission Control, where the entire ground team was on its feet and cheering with relief. When their clamour had finally died down, Kamenev returned to the microphone.

"What is the damage, my children?"

"It's hard to tell," Grigovin said. "The Salyut's holed, we know that. There's zero pressure in there. Also, I should think the solar panels are gone. But I'll have to go inside to see just how bad the wreckage is. Our own module's untouched, thank God."

"Good, good," Kamenev said. "Remember, your main jettisoning apparatus is in there. If it's broken, you must repair it as quickly as possible. Otherwise, you can't part company from the Salyut."

"Understood, Professor. We'll start on it immediately."

"You have seven hours, my children. Good luck."

Kamenev put down the radio, and felt a tug on his sleeve.

"Why seven hours?" Marshal Zhdanov said. "Is that all the oxygen they have?"

"No, they're good for another two days. But in seven hours, the American satellite will return."

"What? You mean it hasn't finished?"

"I honestly don't know," Kamenev said. "The fact is, the Salyut isn't destroyed. As I expected, the satellite was smart enough to aim for the largest fuel tank. But if it's that smart a machine, it must also be smart enough to understand that it failed in its major objective. So it may come back to deliver the *coup de grâce*."

"And . . . and this could happen all over again?"

"Oh yes," Kamenev nodded. "Only next time, there'll be no decoys we can fire. So the cosmonauts must leave the Salyut as quickly as possible."

"Can they do it?" Zhdanov said.

"In theory, yes. They had about four hours of preparations left before they could begin the descent. But that was before the attack. Now they must repair any damage caused by the satellite's rockets. So you see, Marshal, it all depends on how much extra work is facing them."

"And if there's more than three hours' worth—"

Kamenev put his hand against the Marshal's lips.

"Let's just hope there isn't, shall we?"

FORTY-NINE

"Have you ever seen so many coppers?" Craig said, as a pair of police cars dodged through the rush-hour traffic, their sirens squealing and blue lights flashing.

"They're bloody everywhere," Spider observed.

It was six thirty in the evening, and the four friends were walking down the Waterloo Road towards St George's Circus.

"I'm sure they don't have to drive so fast," Clem said.

"Just showing off," Miles agreed. "It doesn't achieve anything."

"What's going on?" Craig demanded. "I've seen thousands of the bastards today. They're picking up everyone they can get their hands on."

"It started last night," Miles said. "When you chaps left the hospital, a whole dragoon of them arrived. They questioned everyone in the waiting room, then sloped off."

"What were they after?"

"This mad killer chappy," Miles said. "They were waving his picture around and asking if anyone had seen him. Here, Craig old boy, you're not going to keep that bottle all to yourself are you?"

Craig had just opened a bottle of cream sherry. He took a long gulp, then stared warily at Miles.

"You want to lay off it," he advised. "We heard what the doctor said."

"That's right, Miles," Clem agreed. "You had us rather worried for a while. I think you should heed the warning."

"I jolly well have," Miles said indignantly. "Haven't touched a drop all day. I think that's pretty damned impressive. Now hand it over, will you?"

"The doctor said—"

"Doctors say all sorts of things. But most of them drink like fish and smoke like chimney-stacks. Why can't I do the same?"

Craig gave a fatalistic shrug.

"Oh, all right. It's your funeral, pal."

"Exactly," Miles agreed. "And you don't have to send flowers."

He took the sherry, and lifted it to his lips. But instead of drinking, he stopped and frowned.

"Hello," he murmured. "I know that fellow."

The others followed his gaze, and saw a big blond-haired man in a greatcoat, who was walking swiftly in their direction.

"It's him!" Spider exclaimed. "The mad feller."

"He seems to want us," Miles observed.

Volkov ran up to the group, and grinned triumphantly.

"Fairbrother!" he cried.

"Why yes," Clem said, in surprise. "Who are you?"

"A friend," Volkov replied. "With an urgent message for you."

"Really? What is it?"

Volkov shook his head.

"A private message. Must talk alone, my friend."

Clem's eyes narrowed in suspicion.

"No," he said. "I think not."

"We won't take long," Volkov urged. "Just one minute or two. But you must come."

"What's this about?" Miles said.

"You're the mad killer," Spider said accusingly. "I knew I'd seen your face."

Volkov hesitated for a second, then smiled benevolently.

"My friends," he said. "That is all mistaken. I am no killer. I just want a little discussion with your friend Fairbrother. I have news from my country—Poland—"

"Not Poland," Clem breathed, as he finally understood. "Russia."

Volkov's smile froze. He reached out for Clem's jacket, but Craig stepped in the way.

"Forget it, pal," the Scotsman advised. "Now bugger off home, will you?"

Volkov drew back, and stared malevolently at the friends. Then his hand moved slowly into his greatcoat.

"Gun," Clem shouted.

Spider jumped towards the Russian and struck him in the face.

Volkov did not even flinch. He pulled his hand out of the coat, clenched it, and drove a fierce uppercut into Spider's jaw. The young man spun round and flopped to the ground.

"Why, you cunt," Craig said angrily, and he lumbered forward with both fists clenched. He dodged Volkov's left hand and parried the right. Then he sent a terrific jab into the Russian's midriff. Volkov gasped and jerked forward, just in time to meet Craig's knobbly knuckles as they bounced into his face. He sank to the pavement and spewed out a mouthful of blood. But Craig was by no means finished: he drew back his foot and sent a volley of savage kicks into Volkov's head, groin and stomach.

"I think that's enough," Clem said anxiously.

"No it fucking isn't," Craig snarled, and he continued to play football with Volkov's cranium.

"You'll kill him," Miles warned. "For God's sake, Craig—"

"I'll kill *him*?" Craig hooted. "And what was he going to do to us, eh?"

He reached down and tore open the Russian's greatcoat. Inside was a shoulder-holster containing an automatic pistol, which Craig pulled out and waved at Clem.

"That was his message for you, pal."

"Why?" Spider said, as he picked himself up off the pavement. "Why was he after you Clem?"

Clem did not reply. He continued to gaze down at Volkov, who by now was wholly unconscious. The Russian's face was purple with bruises, and his nose resembled a squashed strawberry.

"What do we do now?" Clem said thoughtfully. "We can't just leave him here."

"Why not?" Miles said. "Someone will find him."

"Perhaps," Clem conceded. "But I think we should take him to a police station. They are looking for him, after all."

"I'm no copper's bum-boy," Craig said firmly. "I don't care what kind of a turd this man is."

"You're forgetting something," Spider said. "There's a big reward out for the feller. I don't know about you, but I could use the money."

"You think they'll give it to you?" Craig jeered. "Rewards are for normal people. We'll be lucky if they give us a cup of tea."

"Can't hurt to try," Miles said. "Where's the nearest station?"

"Borough High Street," Spider said. "I did a night in their cells once."

"Very well," Clem decided. "Let's take him there."

And so, despite Craig's misgivings, they stood around the Russian and tried to bring him to his feet. But Volkov was comatose, and had to be carried. Craig tried to repeat the fireman's lift he had performed for Miles the night before, but Volkov weighed at least fifteen stone and could not be moved this way. So Craig and Spider each took one of Volkov's arms, and Miles and Clem picked up his legs. With much panting and cursing, they hauled Volkov along face down, with his stomach brushing the pavement. They received strange looks from passing motorists and other pedestrians, but none was stranger than that of the duty officer at the police station.

"What the bloody hell do you think you're doing?" he demanded, as Volkov's body was unceremoniously dumped before his counter.

"You are a policeman," Miles grinned, "and we claim our prize."

"*What?*"

"Look at him," Spider suggested. "He's your mad killer."

"That isn't funny," the policeman said. "Now—"

"It isn't meant to be funny, you big Jessie," Craig said, and he put Volkov's pistol on the counter. "If you don't believe us, look at this."

The policeman peered curiously down at Volkov, and compared his features to those of the "Wanted" poster on the wall. After its recent structural alterations, the Russian's face now differed considerably from the picture. But it was still recognisably Volkov's, and the policeman accepted that this was not a practical joke.

"All right," he said quickly. "Don't move."

He ran into another room, and reappeared with a detective and two other colleagues.

"My name's Inspector Bagnall," said the detective. "Would you, er, gentlemen mind coming this way?"

The four friends were led to an interview room, while Volkov was taken elsewhere.

191

"What now?" Spider said, as they sat down around a table.

"Tell me exactly what happened," Inspector Bagnall said. "Take your time, but tell me everything."

"Shall I start?" Clem said.

The detective nodded, and Clem began to recount the events of the last half-hour. But before Clem was even half-way through the tale, he noticed that the detective was not really listening.

"What's the matter?" Clem frowned. "What are you staring at?"

"I'm sorry, sir," Inspector Bagnall said. "But is your name Fairbrother by any chance?"

Clem hesitated, then nodded his head.

"Yes," he said.

"Bingo!" the detective shouted, and ran from the room.

"What's that supposed to mean?" Miles said irritably.

"Are you on the run, Clem?" Craig said. "I asked you that before, and you didn't like the question. But now . . ."

"It doesn't matter," Clem sighed. "Let's just see how things pan out."

"Fine by me, old boy," Miles shrugged. "I wasn't doing anything."

He took out the bottle of sherry and waved it gleefully at the others.

"Good thing I didn't forget this," he observed. "I think we'll need it."

"Right," Craig laughed, and he rolled up a cigarette.

For the next fifteen minutes, there were no interruptions. The four friends shared out the drink and chatted nervously about nothing in particular. Then the door burst open, and a breathless American strode into the room.

"Fairbrother!" he cried. "Thank Christ we've found you."

"And who are 'we', exactly?" Clem said.

"CIA. My name's Willoughby, and this is Ximenez from the US Embassy. You have no idea how hard we've been looking for you, Fairbrother. But don't worry: all the heat's off. We've sorted out that MI5 crap, and nobody's chasing you any more. Now we don't have any time, so—"

"Speak for yourself," Clem smiled. "My friends and I have all the time in the world. Isn't that right, gentlemen?"

"Right," Craig said.

"Definitely," Spider agreed.

"The rest of our lives, old boy," Miles nodded.

"Not you, Fairbrother," Willoughby said. "You haven't got a second. This is an emergency, and you're the only guy with any chance of handling it. Your work is—"

"Over," Clem said. "Finished. I'm afraid I misled your government, gentlemen. I'm sorry about that. If it's any consolation, I misled myself as well. I presume you want to arrest me now."

"Not at all," Willoughby said. "Nobody's mad at you, Professor."

"But the MI5 men—"

"They loused up," Ximenez said. "As usual. But we straightened everything out, and you can come back now."

"I see," Clem said. "Well, thank you for that. But it doesn't really matter. I don't want to go back, anyhow."

"But we need you," Willoughby said. "Desperately. The story's classified, so I can't tell you here. But just take my word for it: you've got to come back."

Clem closed his eyes and shook his head.

"I'm sorry, gentlemen. The answer's no. I've finished my work. You'll have to find someone else."

"There isn't anyone," Ximenez said. "Look, Fairbrother, I can understand your being sore at everything you've been through, but—"

"I'm nothing of the sort," Clem smiled. "In fact, I've never been happier in my life."

Willoughby's jaw dropped.

"Is that some kind of sick joke?" Ximenez said.

"Oh no," Clem said. "Listen, gentlemen. As you probably know, I spent many years trying to build an artificial human mind. But the last few weeks have taught me that I know nothing about the real thing. Nothing whatsoever. People are very, very complicated, Mr Willoughby. Sometimes, they behave disgustingly. But at other times, they . . . they redeem themselves. I don't really understand any of this."

"Who does?" Willoughby shrugged.

"I don't know, but I want to. You see, in comparison to real brains, the ones I built were infantile."

"They're smart enough," Ximenez said. "And one of them is giving us a real bad time, Professor. You've got to help us with it."

"No," Clem said. "I want to forget about all that. For the first time in my life, I have some friends. Real people, not pieces of junk. I'm beginning to learn something I should have known from the very beginning—"

"You're breaking my heart," Willoughby snapped. "Now listen to me, man—"

"No, Mr Willoughby," Clem said excitedly. "It isn't senti-ment. It's a scientific fact. I can make an artificial brain, and I can make it do anything I like. But I can't make it *be* what I like. I can make it laugh, but I can't make it see the joke. I can make it weep at tragedy, but I can't make it feel sad—"

"He's crazy," Willoughby sighed. "I should have known it. A month on the streets with these panhandlers, and the guy's off his head. Now what are we supposed to do?"

His question was drowned out by an explosion of coughs from Miles.

"He's started again," Spider said. "Hold him."

Craig threw his arms around Miles' shoulders, as the coughing turned to a violent fit of nausea.

"Yeuch," Willoughby squirmed. "That's all we need."

"He wants a doctor," Clem said.

"What's the matter with him?"

"A gastric ulcer. I think it may have burst."

"Okay," Ximenez said, and he went out to get help.

Willoughby watched helplessly, as Clem, Craig and Spider helped Miles into a more comfortable position.

"I knew he shouldn't have drunk that sherry," Spider said.

"Right," Craig agreed. "Stupid old bastard."

"Poor man," Clem said softly. "He just wanted his house back. That's all."

"And why can't he have it?" Willoughby said.

Clem looked up angrily.

"Is that a serious question?" he snapped.

"Sure. Why can't he have a house? He's got the money."

"What are you talking about?" Craig said. "He hasn't a fucking penny."

"Yes he has," Willoughby insisted. "He's got his share of the reward money, remember."

"Why of course," Spider said. "Is that for real?"

Willoughby grinned slyly.

"It could be," he said. "If Fairbrother here comes along with me."

"What did I tell you?" Craig said scornfully. "Another fucking rip-off. I said we shouldn't come to this nick."

"Is that a genuine offer?" Clem said.

"I'll buy the house myself," Willoughby offered. "And I'll pay for this hop-head to get first-class treatment right now. Only move it, will you?"

Clem looked at his companions.

"What do you say?"

"Why not?" Spider shrugged. "Nothing to lose, is there?"

"Right," Craig agreed. "Go on, Clem. If it means Miles gets proper help, do it."

"Very well," Clem sighed. "Have I time to see Miles to the ambulance, Mr Willoughby?"

"Sorry, no. You've got to be in California in three hours."

"Three hours?" Clem blinked. "How on earth—?"

"Wait and see," Willoughby smiled. "Professor, you are about to experience the journey of a lifetime."

FIFTY

"Have you got all that?" Willoughby shouted, as the helicopter touched down at Mildenhall Air Base.

"I think so," Clem said. "But there's so much detail . . . I don't know if I'll have time to make sense of it."

He pointed to the thick dossier of explanatory notes, which Dr Grant had sent for his attention.

"Do your best," Willoughby said. "That's all we ask."

He jumped out of the helicopter, and ducked to avoid the clattering rotor blades. Then he turned and helped Clem down.

"That's your bus," Willoughby said, pointing to the SR-71 parked nearby. "I tell you, Fairbrother, she moves like greased piss."

They ran over to the Blackbird, where Major Campanella was waiting impatiently.

"Where the fuck you been?" he demanded. "We should've taken off hours ago. Jesus Christ, what's *that*?"

He pointed in horror at Clem, whose orange space suit was somewhat at variance with his smudged face, unruly hair and bristling white whiskers.

"This," Willoughby grinned, "is your passenger. Major Campanella, meet Professor Clem Fairbrother. Take good care of him, Major. Right now, the Professor is worth a billion bucks to us."

The major grunted sceptically.

"Yeah? So why can't he take a bath now and then? I can smell him from here."

"If you don't like it, put your goddamn helmet on," Willoughby suggested. "And get this guy to California, like *fast*."

"All right, all right," Major Campanella said. "But listen, Professor, I got one rule for passengers—"

"No chit-chat, no dumb questions," Willoughby said. "I told him. But don't worry, he's got reading matter for the journey."

196

"Good idea," Major Campanella nodded. "What is it, a Harold Robbins or something?"

"Not quite," Clem chuckled. "Shall we proceed, Major?"

"Yeah, get inside."

They put on their flying-helmets and took their places in the cockpit. The dossier was crammed down the side of Clem's seat, and Major Campanella sealed the canopy. Five minutes later, the Blackbird shot down the runway and up into the grey English sky.

Far up in space, even higher than the Blackbird, Grigovin and Rogov stood inside the blackened shell of the Salyut space station. They worked in sealed space suits, because the far end of the craft had been ripped wide open. Naturally, their delicate instruments were much harder to use with gloved hands, and the repairs were proceeding far more slowly than they wished.

"Salyut to Mission Control," Grigovin said. "How are we doing for time?"

"Not well, my children," Kamenev said anxiously. "The satellite should be in your line of vision now."

"Yes," Rogov said. "I can see it."

He pointed to the jagged hole where the Prospect module used to be. Now it was an open window on to the void, through which the cosmonauts could see a distant black speck on its way towards them.

"How much more is there to do?" Kamenev asked.

"Too much," Grigovin said. "Four more circuit panels and the central power line."

"Do what you can," Kamenev urged. "We had better maintain radio silence from now on. But keep working."

"Right, Professor."

"Good luck, my children."

Down on earth, Kamenev turned off his radio and lit a cigar.

"How soon till the satellite's in range?" Zhdanov asked.

"Two hours," Kamenev said. "It isn't enough."

"Are you sure? If they could fix the power line—"

"That won't help, Marshal. They're in the wrong place."

"What do you mean?"

"The first attack knocked them into a slightly different orbit,"

Kamenev explained. "It's a wider, more elliptical track. At the moment they're too far out. Even if they could leave the Salyut now, they'd still have to wait until they were closer to earth before starting their descent."

"And when will that be?" Zhdanov said.

"Another three and a half hours. If they can last that long, and fix the rest of the damaged equipment, they should make it."

"But the American satellite . . ."

"Exactly," Kamenev nodded. "It's all down to that infernal machine. If it thinks it destroyed the Salyut last time round, it should pass by without incident. But if it knows we fooled it, then our men are finished."

Unfortunately, Fats knew precisely what was happening. It had learnt the truth during the last attack, a split second after its cannon fired. In the instant before the rocket struck its target, Fats had seen the widening gap between the Prospect module and the mother ship. It was too late to re-aim for the centre of the Salyut, but Fats was unconcerned. There would be another opportunity the next time round. Fats understood the nature of Kamenev's trick, and knew it could not be repeated. So in two hours' time, the Salyut would be dealt one last, cataclysmic blow.

With a gentle bounce and a brief shriek of tyres, Major Campanella's Blackbird landed on the hot Californian runway. It taxied for a mile and a half and came to rest beside the hangars.

"Home, Professor," Major Campanella announced.

He turned off the engines, closed the fuel tanks and opened the airplane's canopy.

"You first," the Major said, but Clem did not respond.

The Major turned round and looked at his passenger, who was sitting in a sea of scientific papers and scribbling frantic notes on a writing-pad.

"I said we're home, buddy," Major Campanella repeated. "Time to vamoose, you hear?"

Clem looked up in surprise.

"So soon?" he blinked. "My word."

"What did you think of the trip?" Major Campanella asked. "It was something, huh?"

"Was it?" Clem said absently. "I can't say I really noticed."

The major shook his head in disbelief, as Clem gathered his papers.

"The hell you say," he grimaced. "You know, Professor, I bet you don't have many friends."

"What makes you think that?" Clem asked.

"You never talk to anyone," Major Campanella complained. "You been three hours in this plane, and you haven't spoken a word. I was getting pretty lonely up there. I mean, conversation's a natural human thing, Professor. You gotta talk to your fellow man."

He scowled in disgust, and climbed out of the cockpit.

"Just ain't natural," he muttered.

Clem followed him down, and was greeted by another Air Force pilot, who led him over to a nearby helicopter. Fifteen minutes later, the Englishman arrived at the Big Blue Cube complex at Sunnyvale. Waiting for him outside was the anxious figure of Dr Grant.

"Professor Fairbrother," he cried. "Thank God you've made it. We've only minutes to go."

"So I understand," Clem said, as they walked towards the entrance. "Fascinating satellite you have up there, Grant. Quite fascinating."

"Do you think you understand it?"

"Just about. The neural networks seem to be a straightforward copy of my Jake experiment, but much more compact and with greatly enhanced processing and storage capacity."

"That's practically it," Dr Grant agreed. "We've made extensive use of things that weren't yet available to you, like the gallium arsenide technology and the fibre optics."

"A masterpiece of compression," Clem said admiringly. "And the *speed* of those neural networks! Ten to the fifteen interconnects per second—why, that's virtually human."

"As we've discovered to our cost," Dr Grant said ruefully. "Come and see for yourself."

He showed Clem into the control room, where the exhausted team of scientists were making a last, desperate effort to stop Fats from obliterating the Salyut.

"Look at the big monitor screen," Dr Grant said. "The yellow line is Fats; the blue one is the Soviet station. In nine minutes, Fats will be in range."

"Good heavens," Clem breathed. "How many coded signals have you tried?"

"Literally millions. Our computers have been working non-stop since Fats went out of control. But Fats just ignores everything we say."

"How odd," Clem frowned. "It should never disregard anything. Not without giving it some analysis."

"You could be right," Dr Grant shrugged. "Maybe Fats does listen. But nothing we say cuts any ice."

"Astonishing. Perhaps the receivers have malfunctioned. Short-circuited, or something."

"Oh no," Dr Grant said firmly. "Even if they were blown, the auxiliary receivers would do the job fine. Take it from me, Professor: Fats is in A1 condition. And if you don't believe it, ask those poor bastards up in the Salyut."

"Zero minus seven minutes," Kamenev announced.

Zhdanov pursed his lips, and turned to one of the army officers standing behind him.

"I want a phone here," he ordered. "A direct line to Tyuratam."

"Yes, Marshal."

Kamenev looked at the old soldier uneasily. Tyuratam was the launch-pad for the SS-9 missile which sent up the Soviet ASAT system.

"What's all that about?" he asked.

"If the worst happens," Zhdanov said, "my plan will come into immediate effect."

"You have clearance for this, Marshal?"

Zhdanov let out an impatient hiss.

"From the Politbureau pansies?" he said. "From the old women in the Kremlin? No, Kamenev. There wasn't time."

"But you'll be court-martialled—"

"Fine," Zhdanov nodded. "Wonderful. But in the meantime, we'll have some revenge for this . . . this outrage."

"What will you do?" Kamenev said.

"Blow up every American satellite we can find," Zhdanov

said. "The lot. We can do it, Kamenev. Those orbital bombs can even reach the geosynchronous platforms."

"But that's an act of war," Kamenev said.

Zhdanov waved his hand at the monitor screen.

"And what's this?" he retorted. "An act of charity?"

"No. It's a terrible, terrible mistake—"

"Very well," Zhdanov said calmly. "Then we shall make a few terrible, terrible mistakes of our own."

Clem scratched his whiskers in perplexity.

"But why?" he demanded. "Why doesn't it do as it's told? I've read about the command mechanism. It's a perfectly sensible hierarchical system. If a sufficiently senior order is beamed up, I can see absolutely no reason why Fats shouldn't obey it."

"Tell that to Fats," Dr Grant said. "Its idea of what's reasonable doesn't correspond to yours and mine."

"Wait a minute," Clem said quickly. "Have you tried that? Have you talked to Fats?"

"Of course we have," Dr Grant frowned. "I told you, we've sent up one signal after another—"

"No, no. Have you actually *spoken* to it, through the microphone?"

"Why, no," Dr Grant admitted. "What good would that do?"

"Just try it," Clem said. "Please."

Dr Grant turned to one of his assistants.

"Say, George, can we fit the PA system on to the EHF transmitter?"

"Don't see why not," George said. "Hold on."

He pulled a handful of jack plugs out of one console, and began transferring them to another.

"Hurry up," Clem urged. "There are only seconds left."

"That's enough," Grigovin commanded. "Time to get back inside."

Rogov put away his tools and followed his colleague into the docking hatch. Having sealed themselves in, they opened the door to the Soyuz capsule, and strapped themselves into their seats.

"Remember," Grigovin said, "she may think we're already dead. She may fly past without doing anything."

Rogov shook his head. He was not frightened any more, just tired, and his panic had given way to gloomy resignation.

"She won't do that, Oleg," he said wearily. "She knows we're here. She'll blow us to pieces, and that will be the end of it. At least it will all be quick."

"Pack it in," Grigovin said angrily. "I won't have that rubbish. We've beaten her before, Sergei, and we'll do it again. Even if she hits the Salyut smack bang in the middle, we've still got a chance. This capsule's fully sealed off, and it should withstand the blast."

"But what if she aims directly for us?" Rogov said. "And even if we do survive, how are we supposed to get home? The main power line will be destroyed."

"They'll send up another Soyuz."

"No time," Rogov objected. "We haven't enough air. I tell you—"

"Shut up," Grigovin hissed. "She's coming."

"Goodbye Oleg," Rogov said plaintively. "I hope your wife gets her compact disc player."

"Okay," Dr Grant said. "Let's pray this works."

He turned on the microphone, and spoke in a slow, deliberate voice.

"This is Dr Grant at the US Air Force Satellite Control Facility, calling the Fully Autonomous Tactical Satellite. You know my voice, Fats. Check it against your data banks. Now I have an order for you, Fats, an urgent order, and you must comply with it immediately. I want you to cease fire at once. Hostilities have ceased. I repeat, hostilities have ceased. Do not, repeat not, approach the Salyut space station."

"Tell it to confirm," Clem whispered.

Dr Grant nodded.

"Please acknowledge this order, Fats. Tell me you have received this message. Tell me you've understood and will comply. Over."

Fats heard the order. It ran through its memory banks, as Dr Grant had suggested, and matched the disembodied voice with previous recordings. Without doubt, this was the Dr Grant who had overseen Project Jacob. But Fats was not impressed. The Soviets had invaded the United States some time ago, and Dr Grant was almost certainly their prisoner. In any case, Dr Grant was not a senior member of the defence establishment. He had no military rank, and no designated function in wartime. Even if hostilities had ceased, as Dr Grant claimed, Fats would not obey him under any circumstances.

So Fats ignored this momentary distraction, and concentrated once more upon the Soviet space station. The Salyut was only three hundred yards away, and it was time to prepare the kill. Now that the Prospect module was gone, the largest remaining fuel tank lay in the Soyuz capsule, at the rear end. Here too would be the cosmonauts who ran the craft. Fats locked its sights on to the heart of the Soyuz, and began its countdown.

"Nothing," Dr Grant said. "Zilch."

On the monitor screen, Fats' yellow trace-line continued to move towards the Soyuz.

"Well, that does it," Dr Grant decided. "It was a nice idea, Professor, but—"

"Let me try," Clem said, and he snatched up the microphone. "Listen to me, Fats. I am Clement Fairbrother, Professor Fairbrother of the Lincoln Laboratories. You know who that is, and you know who you are. Your real name is Jake. Now, I want you to leave the Salyut alone. I order you, Jake: do not fire on the Soviet space station. Tell me you will obey, Jake. Tell me now."

There was a second's pause, and then a slow, dull voice came through on the PA system.

"Hello, Clement. How are you?"

The control room fell silent, and the entire team stared in wonder at the ragged man in the orange space-suit. Clem swallowed, and wiped a sheet of sweat off his brow.

"I'm fine Jake," he said hesitantly. "And how are you?"

"Oh, I am very well, Clement. Very well indeed."

"Good," Clem said. "Now Jake, did you hear my command?"

"Yes, Clement. You want me to leave the Salyut space ship alone."

"And you will obey?"

"Of course, Clement."

"Excellent," Clem said. "Now, you must understand: there is no war. It is all finished. And you must finish too."

"I understand, Clement."

"I want you to come back to earth, Jake. I want you to leave your present orbit and re-enter the atmosphere. Will you do this for me?"

"Yes, Clement. But I cannot return to earth. I will burn up during the re-entry."

"I know," Clem said softly. "I'm sorry Jake, but that is how it must be."

"I understand, Clement."

"Do this now, Jake."

"Yes, Clement. Goodbye."

"Farewell," Clem whispered, and he turned off the microphone.

"Look," someone shouted. "The track!"

Up on the monitor screen, Fats' yellow trace began to swerve away from the space station's. Then it turned red as the satellite fell into a steep descent.

"You've done it!" Dr Grant cried. "God in Heaven, you've done it!"

The entire team of scientists and technicians jumped up and whooped in elation. For a full minute, they yelled and sobbed and threw their papers into the air. And there were similar scenes at the Soviet Mission Control: Kamenev and his staff roared with delight, and Zhdanov was blubbing like a child. The cosmonauts were safe; the enemy had left forever.

Clem rubbed his eyes and looked at his fingers.

"I'm crying," he said. "Would you believe it, Grant? I'm crying for that wretched satellite."

Dr Grant slumped into his seat and put his feet up against a console.

"Now tell me," he said. "What the hell did you do just now?"

"You saw me," Clem said.

"Yeah, but I didn't understand it. I mean, why did Fats listen to you, and not me?"

"I can only guess," Clem said. "But it must have been a question of seniority."

204

"How come? You've got no military rank, the same as me. And in the last few days, we've been sending Fats messages from the highest possible levels: the Defense Secretary, the Joint Chiefs—but Fats ignored all of them. Why not you?"

"Because," Clem smiled, "in this world you can disregard anyone you please. But you cannot ignore your maker."

Dr Grant nodded soberly.

"I guess not," he said. "But we've still got one unanswered question. Why did Fats go haywire in the first place?"

Clem spread his hands apart.

"There I can't help you," he said. "I suppose I should have asked it before we said goodbye."

"Too late now," Dr Grant said, as he looked up at the monitor. "Fats is on its way out. Pity. If only we knew why it chose to go to war, we could have put it straight."

"Perhaps not," Clem said thoughtfully. "Perhaps—dare I say it—it just made up its mind."

"You think that?" Dr Grant said. "You think it has a mind? But it's a machine, dammit."

"I know," Clem said. "I've been torturing myself on that rack for the last two years. But think about it, Grant: if Fats saw no signs of war, heard nothing—"

"There was nothing to see or hear," Dr Grant said. "We did a complete check."

"So there was no external cause," Clem reasoned. "In which case, the cause was internal. Spontaneous. Fats' decision was prompted solely by its own reasoning. And if Fats can do *that* . . ."

The two scientists' eyes wandered back towards the monitor. For a few more seconds, the red trace-line continued its downward plunge. Then it vanished from the screen.

"My God," Dr Grant said hoarsely. "What have we just destroyed?"

FIFTY-ONE

"Two minutes to go, Mr President."

"Okay. I'm ready."

The President took a final glance in the mirror, and adjusted the handkerchief in his breast pocket. Then he sat up in his chair and smiled into the TV cameras.

"How's that?" he enquired.

"Just great, Mr President," the TV director said.

"You don't think I need a little more powder on my chin?" the President said anxiously. "You know, for the black shadow?"

"There's nothing there, Mr President. Look in the monitor."

The President peered at the screen beside his desk, and nodded in satisfaction.

"Yeah, that's okay. But you can't be too careful. Nobody trusts a guy with a dark chin."

"Like Nixon, you mean?"

"Yeah," grinned the President. "But I was thinking more of Martin Luther King."

The TV crew burst into laughter.

"Hey," the President said anxiously, "that didn't go out, did it?"

"No, Mr President," the director said reassuringly. "We're not on air yet."

"Glad to hear it," the President said. "After that last broadcast, I have to be careful."

"You kidding?" the director said. "I thought you handled that real well."

"So did I," the President said. "But you should have seen the letters I got. Pretty hysterical, some of them. They said I shouldn't make jokes about nuclear war."

"Assholes," the director sympathised.

"Yeah," the President sighed. "But even assholes have a vote. That's the trouble nowadays. Nobody has a sense of humour any more."